THE DAMNED DON'T DIE

All Black Lizard titles are available direct from the publisher or at your local bookstore.

Watch out for the Black Lizard!

THE DAMNED DON'T DIE

by Jim Nisbet

(Original Title: *The Gourmet*)

Black Lizard Books

Berkeley • 1986

The Damned Don't Die was originally published in 1981 by
Pinnacle Books under the title *The Gourmet*.

This first Black Lizard Books edition published 1986.

Black Lizard Books are published by Creative Arts Book Company.
For information contact: Creative Arts, 833 Bancroft Way, Berkeley,
California 94710.

Typography by QuadraType.

ISBN 0-88739-004-8
Library of Congress Catalog Card No. 85-73607

Manufactured in the United States of America

Chapter One

The ecstatic moans from the apartment next to his kept Herbert Trimble awake, but they gave him, as he lay in bed listening, an idea for a story. It would be the best trash story he'd ever written. All he had to do was get up out of bed, walk to his desk, sit down to his typewriter, and begin. There was even a sheet of paper already in the machine; it was blank, and it was rolled down under the platen and back up about 3½ inches, just the proper distance from the top of the page at which to begin an opening paragraph.

I've always wanted to skin a woman.

He'd seen Ms. Sarapath many times and wasn't surprised at the noise from next door, though she'd never, to his knowledge, expressed her orgasms like this before. At least, not since she'd moved into the apartment adjacent to Herbert's. It was true that Herbert thought Ms. Sarapath to be possessed of an unusual beauty, a very dark, smoldering, full-lipped Levantine beauty of the sort that undoubtedly caused Ms. Sarapath a great deal of trouble on the streets of San Francisco, even on the nicer streets, and that it was to this beauty's great attractions Herbert laid responsibility for this long night of aural lubricities. She just can't help herself, he thought, over and over again. Some stud has her pinioned against the wall in there, between the refrigerator and the water heater, a man whose single purpose in life at this moment—he checked his watch: 2:35 A.M.—this hour and fifty minutes worth of moments, has been to bring to this beautiful, lonely, single, working woman pleasure beyond the imagination of the wildest gossip she has ever heard.

1

Oh, well, Herbert thought to himself as he rolled over again, maybe they'll get married.

That'll cool things off.

The voice coming through the partition ebbed to the soft, modulating hum that had underscored all the other sounds of the evening, sounds that ranged from throaty inhalations of delight to piercing shrieks and groans of the most absolute joy and, possibly, pain. Herbert Trimble's imagination had run amuck in the first hour of this woman's night of nights. He had envisaged all manner of sexual acts, sacred and profane, as it were, pleasures he himself had never experienced, had only heard about or dimly conceived. But as the hours wore on, as the tempo or volume of Ms. Sarapath's vocalizations suddenly peaked in wailing or shrieks, Herbert's mind had taken a different tack. These pleasures were not, after all, his own, they flocked to the experience of a stranger he'd never met. He was sharing Ms. Sarapath's ecstasy with another man; she had given herself to someone else. As he realized this unsettling fact, Herbert Trimble also realized that he'd become accustomed, in the few months he'd not quite known her, to thinking of Ms. Sarapath as his own woman. And now, tonight, here she was, apparently in another man's arms, completely out of control.

He tried to imagine her, this woman who wore very fashionable, revealing clothes, and something on her lips that made them look always wet, and not so much facial makeup that it overwhelmed her features. He envisaged the dark, curly hair that fell to her shoulders; he saw her walking in stockings and high heels. . . . And yet she'd always seemed to him a reserved and quiet woman, who seldom, if ever, spoke to him. He tried to imagine this exquisite, possibly brittle creature *writhing*, in sexual abandon. He tried to picture Ms. Sarapath completely naked—except possibly for her stockings and her little open-toed shoes, a thin, gold ankle chain—arched backward over the forearm of an unidentified man, the two of them standing in the middle of the kitchen or the living room, one of her long legs crooked over the buttocks of this deliberate, expert stranger. . . .

2

Not just truss one up and rape her. I've done that, bondage.
Tied one up. Raped and sodomized her, too. And beaten them.
But to skin one . . .
A neat incision from the . . .

Jesus, I'm sick, Herbert thought to himself. He opened
his eyes. The moaning continued through the wall. These
thoughts . . . They trickled, no, they flowed, they flowed
into his mind, the seeds of narrative borne upon them. Of
course, of course, she wasn't his woman, but the jealousy
was there, or the beginnings of it, just as it must be in small
amounts in any man. But he was a rational man. And if he
wasn't?

I've always wanted to skin a woman.

What a thought. Ugh. But yes, what a thought, hmm.
Not rational, but psychotic. Not brilliant, either, but com-
mercial. Point of view, a point of view worth money. An
insight into a soul among the damned.

From the room next door the steady moaning rose almost
to a scream, then subsided into a strange, continual sobbing sigh. Most disturbing, Herbert thought. I'm sort of
aroused and sort of scared. How am I supposed to discern
the difference between pain and pleasure? He rolled over
on the bed, turning his back toward the offending wall.
They say the two blend and meet somewhere, Herbert
thought. Somehow, somewhere the range of human emo-
tion, of sensation, curves back on itself, and pain becomes
pleasure, or vice versa.

The groaning assumed a tempo, little "ohs" came slowly,
regularly through the wall. A thin layer of sheetrock
thought Herbert, then air, interrupted by a stud here and
there, another piece of sheet rock, perhaps $5/8$-inch thick, a
layer of paint . . . And then a different kind of stud, har-
har, Christ, I'm sleepy . . . Almost indiscernably, the
tempo and volume of the moans slowed, reversed, and
began to increase.

Herbert pulled his pillow over his head. He'd been

3

distracted by this apparent lovemaking next door enough to have long since abandoned the book he was reading (*Secrets of the Great Pyramid*) and he'd gone to bed fully clothed. That had been hours ago. Now the moans came more and more frequently, as if they were being shaken from Ms. Sarapath's body. Herbert rolled over again. Christ, he thought, this guy must really be an expert.

—skin her—

By four o'clock, Herbert Trimble was exhausted. He was half-asleep and irritable. He was put out with the girl next door for having so much fun and for keeping him awake while she was at it. And he almost hated the satyr with her. But somewhere in his brain, just lapping the surface of consciousness, Herbert's new idea coalesced and became the germ of a story. The tireless, nagging brain of the artist, Herbert thought to himself. Without it, where would I be? He picked himself up out of his bed and pulled a sweater over his head, answering his own question: I'd be married, with two kids, a home, money in the bank, beer in the refrigerator. He ruffled his hair, leaned low over the typewriter, the keys bathed in a soft, yellowish light. I probably wouldn't be in divorce court, he thought, moving to the other side of the desk, or in this nerve-wracking, low-rent swingles triplex. He briskly massaged his hair and scalp with the fingertips of both hands. A nice, warped, psychotic tale, he thought, about 3,000 words. He seated himself before his typewriter and drew the chair up under the desk. Harry Feyn at *Brandish* magazine will use it, Herbert decided. And he'll pay me cash for it, that'll be good. So maybe the court won't notice, he laughed to himself, when they attach my income. Lousy fifty bucks.

He typed the first sentence.

Chapter Two

Martin Windrow looked at but did not touch the sheet of paper in Herbert Trimble's typewriter. Upon the page, a single line was typed and, he had to admit, it didn't make things look too good for Herbert Trimble.

I've always wanted to skin a woman.

As he read it, Martin Windrow experienced a second wave of nausea.

I've always wanted to skin a woman.

And with it, Martin Windrow suppressed another familiar urge, the sensation of discovery that always rose in his sternum when he'd found a lead, a vector, a clue. The police had found this clue, too. What would be their direction?

Though it was 11:00 A.M. and sunlight streamed in through the windows and across the desk, the desk lamp was lit. Beneath it, a haze of powder clung to the dark typewriter keys, like pollen on the stamens of a large, rectangular flower.

"You must have gotten prints from both hands off this thing," Windrow said, peering at the distinctive lines and creases in the dust under the light.

"Must have," answered a muffled voice from the closet across the room. Steve "Petrel" Gleason stepped through the door of the closet into the space behind the Murphy bed. From one hand dangled a suit on its hanger. His free hand meticulously searched the corners of each pocket, and pinched seams in the pants cuffs and coat. "Everything's been lifted," he said. "You can touch stuff."

"Who said I wanted to touch anything?"

Petrel shrugged, the hanger hooked around one finger. "Suit yourself, hyuk."

Windrow cast his eye over the papers on the desk. There was a bank statement. Mr./Mrs. Herbert Trimble had $475 in a checking account in a branch bank in a nice neighborhood below Twin Peaks. The statement had been forwarded from an address near the bank to the apartment complex northeast of the Panhandle in which Herbert Trimble kept his typewriter, read his books, stacked his music, and hung his suits.

No one, just now, could say where Herbert Trimble was keeping himself.

"They're looking to make these prints with the ones next door," Gleason volunteered from the closet.

On one corner of the desk a large ashtray containing little cigarette ends and a hemostat held down a neat stack of paper, three inches high. The ashtray, being light in color, was covered with a dark dust, lampblack. Removing the tray, Windrow picked up half of the thick sheaf of typescript, exposing a page numbered 256 in its upper-right corner. He began to read.

" . . . thought that, out of superstitious reverence—in spite of his family's vocation, practiced for generations—for the royal house and its deities—for the boy held, as, indeed, all of Egypt held, these kings to be holy and sacred, and as such protected by those supernumeraries to whom such duties were charged—the child-thief had probably covered the fierce aspect of the guardian uraeus with the cloth to prevent its witnessing the subsequent pillage of the royal sarcophagous. It has been suggested (Schröder, *ibid.*, p. 237) that the boy, not without a certain salacious yet fearful delight, employed his own loincloth for the purpose; but more recent scholarship (Dinwittie, *op. cit.*, p. 342; Chauncey, *Journal of the Proceedings of the British Society of Thanatology*, vol. XLII, no. 2, pp. 178-180) indicates that after appropriate analysis the decomposed textile found upon the cobra's visage is quite similar, if not identical, to the exquisite linen covering the bench upon which the viscera jars are arranged, and much like the cloth used to stuff the body cavities of the mummified. Sanders himself (*20,000 A.D.*, pp. 23 and 24) mentions this material . . ."

Windrow replaced the manuscript. Under its paperweight, in the center of the uppermost page, was neatly typed *The Art of Death*. Windrow stared at the single sheet in the typewriter.

I've always wanted to skin a woman.

Gleason exited the closet and extended his hand, palm up. Upon it rested variously sized and colored tablets and capsules, a square of stiff paper covered with a ruled grid, and a small, greenish brown substance which, except that it glittered with specks of gold, looked like a lump of dirt. Gleason did not attempt to conceal a small note of triumph in his voice. "Our boy's a doper," he said. He stood on the other side of the large, flat desk and pushed the pharmaceuticals around his palm with a corner of the stiff, ruled paper. "All we need now are a few surgical instruments."

Windrow looked at Gleason, and Gleason avoided his eyes. Gleason, who with his slim build, his long trench coat, his gaunt, yellow face, permanently pursed lips, the beak nose between restless, tired eyes, looked uncannily ornithomorphic. It was the demeanor that went with the mind of a man who had eaten a bad breakfast every day for fifteen years and, every one of those days, expected a worse lunch.

Windrow picked up the hemostat from the ashtray on the desk. Its ends were blackened from the matches held to it, and everybody would know that Trimble used it to hold roaches under his nose, and perhaps the noses of his friends, but it was all Gleason needed. "Here."

Gleason stared at the tool for a long time. "Jesus," he finally said, "whadda creep. A hophead with an ax."

Windrow indicated the handful of dope with the hemostat.

7

"You hold on to that stuff long enough, they'll be towing you out of here on a string," he said.

"Huh?"

"Osmosis."

Gleason looked at his hand and jumped. "Jesus, shit," he said. He dumped the evidence out of his hand onto the desktop and rubbed his hand on the breast of his trench coat, smoothing the material over the butt of the cannon suspended underneath.

"Better wash it off," Windrow suggested. Gleason looked at his hand. "Yeah, right," he said and headed for the bathroom. While he was running water over his hand, the phone rang next to Windrow on the desk. It, too, being dark was covered with a light dust.

"Hey, get that," Gleason said over his shoulder.

"Sorry," Windrow answered. "I'm not here, remember?"

"Shit," Petrel said again and came hurrying out of the bathroom drying his hands on his coat.

While Gleason listened to the telephone, Windrow watched the surfaces of the room in which he had found himself. It was the room of the man on whom this morning Windrow had set out to serve papers of divorce, including notification of a court date. Windrow was working for Mrs. Trimble's lawyer. Not a nasty job—though that depended on an individuals' idea of nasty—not nasty exactly, nor particularly demanding. There was never much satisfaction to be expected out of such employment, either, but the unexacting pace would give his system the time and energy it needed to devote to the careful healing of the stitches in his mouth, his abdomen, and his left buttock. And while he'd been getting sewn up, someone had let the air out of his bank account. So he spent his days riding around San Francisco looking for men who weren't trying too hard to hide, who wouldn't try to kill him when he found them, or sue him when they lost the other thing, who might even thank him when they saw what it was he'd come to deliver, and have him stay long enough for a drink. Very quickly he'd made the discovery that Scotch felt better than anything else applied to the sutures on the inside of his cheek, really

8

perfect as it washed over the swollen tissue and stung around the cracked, loose teeth.

So this guy Trimble didn't look like much trouble. Just a potential divorced person who liked to read. He owned a lot of books, big, bound books that lined two walls head-high around the room. Two thirds of them were concerned with eschatology, theology, Egyptology, burial rites, archae ology, astronomy, and embalming, with a smattering of biology, physics, botany, zoology, medicine, and surgery. He couldn't find a single text on psychiatry, psychology, or mental disorders. There was a whole shelf of books on myths and mythology, and a large collection of sheet music, loose and bound, musical biographies, musicology and harmony texts. The rest of the collection seemed to be characterized by a taste for morbid fiction. There was an old and beautiful *Works of Poe* in several vellumed volumes. H. P. Lovecraft, *The Turn of the Screw, La-bas, The Moonstone,* several bound volumes of *Weird Tales* magazine, Lautremont, Baudelaire, Rimbaud, Gogol, Georges Bataille, Harlan Ellison, de Sade, Sacher-Masoch, a book of Bosch reproductions, a book of Francis Bacon reproductions, a shelf of paperback novels whose jacket blurbs characterized them each and all as horrible, macabre, bizarre, chilling, spine-tingling, hair-raising, fantastic, morbid, disgusting, and thrilling.

There were several loose and odd numbers of one *Brandish,* a pulp horror magazine, on a low shelf below the window behind Trimble's desk. Windrow scanned the tables of contents of five of them and noticed that each had in common the name of the editor, Harry Feyn, and the name of one writer, Cam Bastion.

The copy of *Brandish* he was holding had a lurid, colored-newsprint cover, which depicted a pneumatic, orange-haired woman, wearing lipstick and an open kimono, partially enwrapped by the tentacles of a sort of hairy, lonesome-looking red squid, three or four times her size. The monster was so big that he obscured part of the title of the magazine, and his tentacles modestly covered those parts of the woman the kimono should have.

Windrow opened the magazine to Cam Bastion's story, entitled, "Power of Attorney," and read the first line.

Mother, she hasn't been able to leave her room, high up in this old, weathered mansion, for ten years now. I've had to do everything for us, her and me. The food, the bedpan, the TV. Old bitch.

Windrow replaced the magazine on its shelf. He looked again at the typewriter, and the single line on the page it held.

I've always wanted to skin a woman.

The little metal window above the ribbon was aimed at a new line, at least four blank lines below the first line, and beginning directly under the *I* of *I've*. Gingerly, Windrow tested the carriage of the typewriter. It moved easily to the right and stopped, so that the window centered on a space less than an inch to the left of the *I*, about an inch from the lefthand edge of the clean page. Had Trimble typed the first line, doubled spaced, indented, and stopped? Windrow pushed the TAB bar. The carriage slid to the left, until the metal window focused on the space four lines directly below the letter *I* in the first sentence, as before.

Gleason hung up the telephone.

"This guy is a writer," Windrow said, almost to himself. Gleason stared at him.

"No shit, Sherlock." He held up one finger. "That's the first reason he's probably off his nut and walking the streets with a meat cleaver and a bone saw."

Windrow looked up from the page in the typewriter and at Gleason. "Yeah? What's another one?"

Gleason swept his arm to indicate the rest of the room. "He was a student of death, couldn't get enough of it. They found his ex-wife, your client's client. Says he got so interested in the subject he quit his job, two years ago, to devote all his time to it. Then, after they'd moved to the city, he got so weird she threw him out. Says she hasn't seen him since. Wanna guess what that job was?"

10

"Assistant Curator of Amerindian Artifacts, Pamela Museum, Palo Alto."

"Oh, a smart guy."

"Yeah. So he was a museum curator. So what?"

"So he was fascinated by dead things to the exclusion of normal pursuits, like home and wife. He's sitting all by himself in this crummy apartment for six months, all worked up on the subject of death. He's handled buried objects, ancient stuff, been in tombs, measured and excavated burial sites, fingered the bones. But he's never actually witnessed the snuff. Better, he's never actually engineered a snuff. So finally he thinks he'll go out and get a little first-hand experience in the matter."

"He didn't go very far."

"I think he went way too far," said Gleason grimly.

"Then there's the hemostat, you found it yourself. Surgical instrument."

"Hm? Oh, yeah. That's the fourth reason, I guess. The hemo-what?"

"Stat. Stauncher."

"Yeah, nice. Well, I guess he didn't bother to take it with him next door, judging by the look of things over there; but the fifth reason is, he played the cello."

Windrow raised one eyebrow.

"Yeah, the cello. It's in the closet. Highest suicide rate of any desk in the orchestra. A very Edge City tribe, the cellopersons."

"Do you have any vacation coming, Steve?"

"Job's too fascinating."

"Come on, Stevie, you got any evidence? Remember evidence?"

"There's an APB out on the guy. Armed and rabid."

Windrow sighed. "Right, what more do you need."

Gleason shrugged. "Been next door?"

"You know I haven't. You didn't even let the press in." Though not looking forward to it, Windrow had been waiting for this invitation. He was the only man in town who called Petrel Gleason by his first and proper name. This accorded Windrow certain privileges, if you call standing knee-deep in the gore of a fresh murder a privilege.

"Sure. Why not?"

Gleason looked at him.

" 'Cause it's a fucking mess," he said. "That's why not."

Chapter Three

The uniformed cop at the door stepped aside for Petrel and Windrow, permitting himself a fluid elision from an indifferent nod to Petrel through a barely noticeable sneer for Windrow, back to sleepy boredom as he stepped into position again between the front door and a small crowd of neighbors, two reporters, a photographer, and a UPS driver. This small tableau loitered thickly in the hallway between Herbert Trimble's and Virginia Sarapath's apartments.

Once inside, Martin Windrow immediately regretted his having anything to do with Herbert Trimble.

Blood was everywhere, but mainly it clotted a thick dark channel that ran from under the bathroom door to the center of the living room. Some of the fluid had been tracked into the kitchen. There were smudged red handprints and fingerprints on the bathroom door and jamb. Cops were everywhere, or those who worked for the cops.

Glen Miller played "Pennsylvania 6-5000" jauntily, not too loud, on a radio in the sunny kitchen.

Most of the men and even one of the women present smoked smelly cigars. Many of them wore thin latex gloves. The windows were open, and there were flowers wrapped in newspaper on the kitchen table.

Petrel Gleason spoke briefly to one of the other officers and then looked significantly at Windrow. "No trace of Trimble yet." He jerked a thumb toward the bathroom. "Wanna see the set?" He didn't wait for "Not particularly," an answer Windrow considered offering.

"In here." Gingerly avoiding the wet carpet, Windrow followed Petrel into the bathroom. Twisted between the

12

toilet bowl and the tub, extending into the center of the room was a lumpy sheet under which the red river ended. From the end nearest the door extended an ankle and a small, slippered foot. It looked like a badly wrapped present. A small gold chain, with tiny links and a heart-shaped clasp, encircled the leg where the ankle became calf. Except for a lavender cover on the toilet seat and a small pair of sepia curtains on the window, most of the bathroom was white. The walls were painted white, the tile floor was white, the porcelain fixtures were white; with these the blood contrasted brightly. A bloodied straight razor with a black handle lay on the floor of the bathtub.

"She crawled in here, maybe even walked, though I guess she was pretty weak, and got the razor out of the medicine cabinet over the sink. . . ." Gleason's voice trailed off. A different, more clinical voice from behind them took up the narrative. "It's hard to tell, but her wrists were cut, could have been self-inflicted. The rest of the damage . . . no way."

"The rest of the damage?"

"A lot of bruises, some of them sexual-type bruises. But her breast . . . Her wrists she could have cut herself, and it looks like the razor did the wrists no matter who did it, but the breast . . . Here." The man who had been speaking inserted himself into the room between Gleason and Windrow and picked up a corner of the sheet. The floor beneath the sheet was covered in blood, as was the forearm exposed by the medical examiner's movements. The shoulder was pure white, almost as white as the tile underneath it might have been, though tinged with the slightest gray. Though her black, curly hair was matted in blood, her face had not a mark on it, and though the tongue had swollen behind the clenched teeth, Windrow thought that she must have been very pretty.

But the medical examiner pointed to where Ms. Sarapath's left breast had been.

"The left breast has been removed," he said, for the benefit of any blind people who might have been present. He swabbed at the dead woman's chest with a small flat sponge. "See? The job seems to have been done within the last twelve hours; there's no scar tissue. No sutures, either."

Petrel Gleason exhaled through pursed lips. "Clean as a whistle," he said with an obvious air of disbelief. He turned away. "No air in these joints," he said and left.

The coroner's assistant, still holding the corner of the sheet up in the air with one hand and squatting next to the body, looked up at Windrow. Windrow ran his tongue along the sutures in his cheek, counting them absently. When he got to six he started his tongue back toward the front of his mouth, where his eyetooth had started the gash.

"If you were to skin this woman, how would you go about it?"

The coroner's assistant's mouth opened and closed, opened and closed a second time.

"Like a deer?" Windrow persisted. "Would you cut her like you'd cut a deer, or a rabbit? Up the belly to the throat?"

The young man replaced the sheet and shook his head, but said nothing.

"Would you?"

The young man stood up. "Who the fuck are you?" he said. Though there were no sibilants in it, he managed to hiss the question.

"Windrow, private."

The young medical examiner stared at him a moment longer, then said, "Yeah. I guess I would. If I was to want to skin her."

"Any sign of that?"

"None."

Windrow turned and walked into the living room. His first step squished discreetly in the wet carpet, and he side-stepped the next one. He found a dry place on the carpet and scrubbed his foot on it.

"So, still like the smell of police work, eh?"

Windrow looked up from his sawing shoe into a sour, fat face full of wrinkles and said nothing.

14

"Once a cop, always a cop, I guess, no matter how bad," said the face. Windrow continued to scrub his foot in the deep pile of the beige carpet. The shoe left red streaks.

The face didn't let up. "Who let this apple in here?" it demanded in a loud voice. No one said anything. Two technicians continued to quietly dust the kitchen countertop, a duplicate of the one in Herbert Trimble's apartment across the hall. The radio muttered.

"Petrel," shouted the face, still watching Windrow.

Gleason, who had been standing next to the face, watching Windrow's shoe go back and forth in the carpet, said, "Yeah, Max?" in a quiet voice.

"Only police personnel on a homicide, Petrel."

"Right."

"So who's this?"

"Thought it might be a tie-in, Max. He was serving split-script to the kink next door."

"Process server, big deal."

"Well . . ."

"But he's no help, right?"

"Well . . ."

"But we're doing all we can, right?"

"Sure, Max, but . . ."

"His butt, Petrel. Out the door. His this time, next time it'll be yours."

Petrel sighed. "Let's go, Windrow."

Windrow walked past Max, who said, "So long, apple," over his shoulder as he headed for the bathroom. As Windrow approached the door, still looking at his shoe, he ran into a woman.

Her face was a mess, not because of her looks, but because she'd cried all over her makeup, and she was scared. She was tall, dressed sharply, blonde, and her eyes were black, sad, and alert.

Windrow stopped. She was undoubtedly Sarapath. A cousin. Or her mother. But a different sister altogether. She had lines that ran back from her eyes, and features slightly puffed from more than crying, from drinking, maybe. From behind her sadness her eyes focused on him and sized him

15

up, from his eyes down to just above the knees and back again.

"You're about a hundred years off," he said.

"*Sic transit*, buster," she said immediately.

In spite of what he felt had to be the worst circumstances of her undoubtedly interesting life, and the general smell of death, Windrow felt a tiny, dimly familiar thrill. He jerked his head toward the room behind him. "Sister?"

Her eyes misted again, and she looked hard at him through the water. No answer.

"I'm sorry," Windrow said and strode through the door Steve Gleason held open for him.

In the hall two men immediately dogged his footsteps.

"Hey, Windrow!"

Windrow kept walking. He could see the stairhead, half-way down the hall.

"Windrow!" One of the men turned in front of him and stopped blocking his path.

"Windrow what's happened in there? What's your connection with this case? That a dead whore in there?"

"Nothing, none, and no." He started forward again.

"Listen, man, a woman's been murdered . . ." The man put his hand on Windrow's shoulder and pushed. Windrow, whose habitual stride caused him to look down just in front of his feet, stopped. He looked slowly up under the brim of his hat into the man's eyes, then slowly moved his eyes to the man's hand, still on his shoulder.

"I guess they could wire that pencil to your wrist," he said.

After a slight hesitation, the man dropped his hand and moved aside.

Chapter Four

Martin Windrow walked down the street until he came to a bar. He went in and had a drink. The Scotch still felt good on his stitches, so for the second time that day, he did not take one of the pills the doctor had given him. Instead, he had another Scotch.

The Toyota started. At the first traffic light it stalled, and it started again. When they got to Windrow's office, one of several in a building downtown, a few blocks south of Market, the car switched itself off as it drifted into a parking space.

Upstairs, it was three in the afternoon. Time to finish off the day with a few phone calls and a couple of drinks, then dinner and some television. Nothing uproarious, nothing dangerous, nothing exciting. With that part of the doctor's prescription he could go along, at least until the rib healed. The least bit of excitement, like slouching in an aisle seat in an adult movie theater, caused the broken rib to sting and pinch deep inside him. No excitement for a month. That was okay with Windrow, although, he supposed, he had a few ribs left.

He eased himself down into his old swivel chair and pulled a bottle out of the lower drawer, and a glass. When he tried to put his feet up, the stitches in his behind tugged at their moorings, and the rib jabbed. Easy does it. He poured himself a drink, sitting upright, and pulled the telephone answering machine close enough to reverse the tape and switch it to audit.

"Windrow, where the fuck are you? Call me," the first message said. It was Emmy Cohen's voice, the lawyer retained by Mrs. Trimble.

"Win a free electric steak knife. Subscribe to the *Chronicle* or the *Examiner* for just six months and win a free electric steak knife. Our new computer subscriber service is waiting to take your call. Just call us at 666-3434, and leave your name, telephone number . . ."

Windrow looked out the window. Three whores stood in the doorway to a grocery store across the street, looking in three directions. A police car sat in the bus zone on the corner. A Cadillac cruised slowly past the store.

"Windrow. Can I call you Marty? Give me a call at 626-9981. Marilyn Sarapath."

Windrow raised his eyebrows and turned to his desk. Her voice was husky, just a touch slurred. A drinker for sure. He switched off the machine and used the telephone directory. He dialed a number. The other end rang twice.

"Hello?" The voice was husky and peremptory.

"Hello, Mrs. Trimble?"

Silence.

"Mrs. Trimble?"

"What do you want?"

"Mrs. Trimble, I'm Windrow, the man assigned to deliver the subpoena to your husband? You know, your divorce?"

"What do you want?"

Some good advice, Windrow thought. And a small loan. But he said, "Well, ma'am, I'm having trouble locating your husband, and—"

"The police were here an hour ago."

"Yes, ma'am. But I wouldn't worry yourself about that."

"I'm not worried about that. What my husband does with his free time is his business."

That's a liberal thing, Windrow thought, for a divorcée to allow her ex-husband.

"But that doesn't have anything to do with you."

"Of course, Mrs. Trimble. What I need is a recent photograph of your husband, so maybe I can—"

"Why don't you ask the police? They'll have a good one any time now."

"Oh, that may be correct, Mrs. Trimble, but if I can get to him with this subpoena first, why, then your case will have precedence in the courts over any case the police might want to press against him."

"Is that true?"

18

"Yes, ma'am. Not that I think the police have anything on your husband. . . ."

"Oh, yes? What do you know about it?"

Windrow moved the mouthpiece of the receiver enough to take a sip of Scotch. "Nothing, ma'am. I'd just like to get to him first, in the best interest of my client, who is working in the best interests of yourself." The stitches were almost numb now. The voice on the other end of the telephone sighed.

"The police already took away the best shot I had, but I think I can find something a couple of years old around here, or at least a wedding picture."

"How long ago were you married to your husband, Mrs. Trimble?"

"Fifteen years."

"Well, that's just fine, Mrs. Trimble. I'll drop by and get the pix from you. Would this evening be all right with you?"

"I'll be home all night, Mr. Windrow, but please don't come by too late."

"I'll be there before eight, Mrs. Trimble."

She hung up.

Windrow got a dial tone and dialed another number. The phone rang six times.

"Yeah." The voice was hoarse, but no thicker than before. Windrow could hear the years, the bad men, the booze in it.

"Windrow."

"Oh—"

"Your sister know a guy named Trimble?"

"Only by his mailbox."

"Thanks."

"Wait—"

He waited. Down the block a jackhammer started up. The Cadillac cruised by in the opposite direction, slowing in front of the liquor store and the whores. From out of the police car window a milkshake cup fell into the gutter. Thursday didn't wait.

"She was a good kid, Windrow. Straight ahead. Why her

19

and not me? Christ, when I think of the kinks I been with . . ." Her voice trailed off.

"Maybe you can read men like books in the dime rack, honey, but your sister couldn't. Or wouldn't . . . Which was it?" He heard the soft click of ice against glass through the phone. The jackhammer started up again; he hadn't noticed it stop.

"Oh, I don't know, we weren't that close. She was like, she was like everything I wasn't. Had a good job, never got in trouble, paid her taxes, slept with somebody not too important around the office once a week . . ." She sobbed. "Then she, I don't know, she . . . She never would tell me what was going on in her head; I don't know if she was even paying attention to her life. She had this career, she was the first woman accountant with this big company—"

"What company?"

"Oh—P.—ahm, P. A.—P. J. Brodine; it's an accounting firm, you know. People hire them to figure out their book-keeping systems and do the payroll and taxes and stuff."

Windrow wrote "P. J. Brodine" on his pad. "She ever talk to you about her work?"

"Yeah, she'd tell me about the men there, mostly, figur-ing that would be what I was interested in. I mean what do I care about counting beans? There was a guy a couple of desks down thinking about leaving his wife. He never did."

"That over?"

"Yeah, but it took a while. Longer for her than him. It was, like, a beseeching look over the water cooler every day for, oh, I don't know, months. He just quit speaking to her. I guess they slept together about twice. Then, whammo, no contact. Poor girl."

"We all have to learn."

"Oh, tough guy."

Windrow said nothing.

"Listen . . ."

He listened.

"I'm coming apart."

"Yeah. So's the Bay Shore Freeway."

"You son of a bitch. When's the last time your little sister fell into a meat grinder?"

He pinched his sinuses. "Sorry."

Silence. The pneumatic drill had stopped.

"Listen . . . I'd like some help with this. It's pretty bad. They needed somebody to identify her . . ."

Windrow rubbed his forehead.

"Are you—I mean, if you happen to run across this creep . . ." She took a drink. "Do you carry a gun?"

"Sometimes."

"Bring it over here."

"You sure you need that kind of help?"

"Yes. No."

"I see."

"Please . . . ?"

"I'll get there around nine."

She gave him the address and hung up.

Windrow swiveled his chair back around to face his window, gingerly leaned back, and twirled his pencil between the fingers of both hands. The cop car and one of the whores were gone, and as he watched, the Cadillac came back down the street for the third time. Windrow counted the stitches in his cheek with his tongue, forward and backward. Down the hall someone closed a door with a glass panel in it and locked it. Footsteps came down the hall, passed Windrow's office, and faded down the staircase. Eventually, the street door opened and closed, two stories below. Far beyond the buildings, up the street to the west, Windrow could see the leading edge of the fog bank, boiling over and down the slopes of Twin Peaks.

The telephone rang. Windrow reached behind him and picked up the glass of Scotch. The phone rang again. He took a drink. The phone rang a third time and a fourth before he picked up the receiver.

"Windrow, where you been? I been calling all day. Don't you ever call back?"

"I've been out getting shown grisly things."

"Skip the editorial. They found a bloodstain on Trimble's doorknob."

21

"Inside or out?"

"What? How should *I* know? You want to know?"

"Might be something."

"I'll get back to you. But the heat's on Trimble for sure."

"He's all they got."

"Yeah, but unless he comes unglued in front of witnesses, they got no case. Or is there something I don't know?"

"There's nothing you don't know, Emmy. It looked circumstantial to me, but they've hung women for less."

"I'll bet that just tickles you pink."

"Show a little leg in court, I always say."

"No, that's what *I* always say. I just hired the foxiest grad student you ever—or you *might* ever . . . Want to meet her? She's a lot smarter than you are. You might learn something from her, about the law I mean."

"Sure. When I find Trimble I'll give her second crack at him. Unless the cops get to him first, in which case she'll just have to read it in the papers like the rest of us. Has his wife heard anything?"

"I was going to ask you that."

"I guess I'll have to ask her, then. I'm on the way over there, to get visual reconnaissance and a picture. Okay, boss?"

"Get to him first, Marty. Maybe you'll get paid this week."

"Thanks."

Emmy Cohen hung up. Windrow turned back to his window and sipped his Scotch. Then he turned around again. He pulled the typewriter board out from under the desktop and ran his finger down the stained list taped there until he found a number, and dialed it.

"Hiya, Steve. Windrow. Was the blood on Trimble's doorknob inside or out? What? Yeah. No, I'm holding him in a closet in the Filmore until I get my price from the P.E.N. American Center. You in for half?

"It was on the inside knob? Hm. No, nothing." Windrow sat silently for a moment. Gleason told him they'd found Trimble's fingerprints in the Sarapath apartment.

"You haven't found him yet? What type blood? Whad-
daya mean, you don't know? Okay, I'll call back. Right.
If I see him, I'll let you know, the very first thing.
Right. Oh, yeah. I need a pic of the deceased. Can do?
Yeah, yeah. Come on, Stevie. Okay. Great. Yeah. Thanks.
So long."

He hung up and moved to the refrigerator, situated
between the entrance door and the bathroom. Inside, he
thought to himself: So the bloodstain was on the inside of
Herbert Trimble's locked apartment. He opened the refrigerator and looked inside. The first two packages, wrapped
in white paper, he removed and threw into the trash basket
beside the desk without looking into them. He pulled out a
frosted glass, a bottle of dark beer, and an egg. Opening the
freezer compartment he dug two ice cubes from a plastic
bucket and dropped them into the glass. He closed the
doors, humming tunelessly. He carried everything back to
his desk and set it all down on top of his mail, thinking,
well, the future doesn't look too good for old Herbert, no
matter how he fits into this. He poured the two ice cubes
from the frosted beer glass into the nearly empty Scotch
glass. Then he broke the egg into the frosted glass, threw
the shell halves into the wastebasket and, holding the beer
glass up to the light from the outside window, carefully
poured the dark Mexican beer down the side of the glass,
minimizing the head. He drank the remainder of the beer in
the bottle and threw it into the trash. He belched and
walked over to the window. Carefully, so as to avoid the
sutures in his abdomen, he inserted one hand in his trouser
pocket, and contemplated his view. The third prostitute
was back with the others, in the doorway across the street.
Above their heads a couple of doors down the neon silhouette of a pink cocktail glass tilted one way, filled up with
three big, green bubbles, went dark, then tilted the other
way and filled up again.

Windrow turned from the window and retrieved a letter
opener from his desk and, resuming his survey of the
street, stirred the beer and egg. The concoction foamed
considerably, and he had to sip the barm off the rim to keep

it from spilling. With an expansive gesture he toasted the street. "It's a good thing I don't smoke," he said aloud, and quaffed half the beer-and-egg solution. "Ah," he said and turned on an old radio that squatted on top of one of the two file cabinets that stood between the bathroom door and the window hall. A loud hum emanated gradually from it, then, distantly at first, came the tinny strains of an old big band hit from the forties. It got louder, though never as loud as the hum; and Windrow was back at the window and nearly finished with his beer and egg before he recognized the tune. It was Glen Miller's Orchestra, playing "Pennsylvania 6-5000." What had nearly been a smile in Martin Windrow's features decayed into the hard, faraway expression of a man who wasn't seeing what he was looking at, as the fog of late afternoon rolled down Folsom Street, between the town and the sun.

Chapter Five

Mrs. Trimble opened the door wide. "Who is it?" She was not beautiful somehow.

"Windrow . . ."

For just a moment, he was taken aback by her appearance. The bones in her face were too square and she wore too much makeup over them, bizarrely colored. She had blonde, almost white hair that looked permanently bleached and sculpted into its shape. She wore tight, black-leather pants, tied at the ankles, that might have been less revealing than a fluoroscope, but not much. Her blouse was of diaphanous white silk, and she wore a black brassiere under it. The light from the rooms behind her silhouetted the lines of her ribs and her very small breasts and, as she turned aside to let him in, the aureole of a nipple. Around her neck she wore a tight-fitting collar, consisting of chromed, rectangular links about an inch high, each link connected to the next by a stack of tiny metal loops. But even so large and bright a piece of costumery as this necklace could not hide the bruises on her throat, which displayed their extreme edges perfectly when she turned in the hall light. Better to say, Windrow thought, as he brushed past her, that she pivoted to let him in, for the nearly vertical high-heeled shoes on which she'd perched herself permitted little else.

More words jumped into Windrow's mind as he entered the living room. *Lush*, not to say *gracious*, occurred to him immediately. The room was lit by a small reading lamp leaned over the arm of a chair in one corner, and by candle-light everywhere else. Leather-bound books in dark cases lined one wall. The carpet was white and so deep that he thought her shoes might be more practical than he'd first thought. Not that she looked impractical, exactly, he thought again, turning to face his hostess, who'd followed him into the room with the pizzicato gait peculiar to her kind of balancing act.

"Drink?" she said, striding past him to the bottle-covered glass-and-chrome cart on wheels which stood in a corner. She held up an unmarked decanter, one third filled with a dark fluid. Beyond her, through a large sliding-glass door, the city twinkled through wisps of fog. Her earrings dipped in and out of the distant points of light.

"Ah, sure."

With the elbow of the hand that held the drink resting against one prominent hip, she swirled the liquid in the cut-glass decanter. "Brandy?" she said in a voice so full of meaning, so thick with import—and through a smile so lascivious—that Windrow, convinced she couldn't be serious, decided that her tone couldn't convey anything more complicated than a trace of mockery.

Still, he suddenly realized, he'd see this woman in hell before he'd try any of her brandy.

"Scotch," he said. "I'm kind of in a hurry."

Her face collapsed visibly, then buoyed again. She changed bottles and poured five ounces of labeled, good Scotch into an eight-ounce water glass. She held it up. "Ice?"

Taxi, Windrow thought to himself, looking around the room. "Please, ma'am."

He heard two distinct plunks, as if she'd dropped the

25

cubes down a well shaft. She poured herself a discreet slug, without ice, from the jug of cut glass, and walked the drinks over to Windrow.

"Here," she said. It was two or three hours' worth of booze. "Cheers."

They each took a sip. Windrow set his drink down on the low glass tabletop in front of the sofa and put both hands in his front pants pockets, thumbs out. The four fingers of his left hand gently covered the stitches in his abdomen. Mrs. Trimble walked around Windrow and set her drink on an end table next to the black sofa behind him.

"Nice place you have here, Mrs. Trimble," he began, but before he could tack the proper intonation onto the end of this pleasantry, she had him. Expertly, she placed one leg behind his knees and pulled him backward over it.

As they fell to the sofa, he landing on his back, she on his legs, he saw that he had a clear shot at her head. The balled fist of his right hand might easily have knocked her senseless. But having an idea of what she was about, he used his right hand to reach around his back and cushion the impact of the sofa on his sutured buttock, leaving his left hand still covering the abdominal wound. In spite of this precaution, the sutures tugged at his flesh. One or two might have torn loose. As he'd fallen, his stomach muscles had automatically hardened, and the broken rib, constricted by them, jabbed his lung. He exhaled sharply, and his eyes filled with water, through which he looked down his supine torso at the leering, blonde features of Mrs. Trimble. Her smiling mouth was just above her hands, which were on his zipper and what was underneath.

"Honey's the name," she said, unzipping his pants. "My master told me to get as much experience as possible." She rubbed her chest against him; the tip of her tongue flashed along her upper front teeth.

She was voracious. The multiple bracelets on her forearms jangled.

He let her work at it awhile.

Then she rolled her eyes up at him, catching his. He could see no understanding in her eyes, only puzzlement.

How could this fail? She slowed, stopped. Windrow, wincing from another jab in his lung, stood up. The seat of his pants was wet.

"You're no fun." Honey Trimble pouted, sitting back on her heels. Her lips and chin were wet with saliva and did, undeniably, look interesting. Though still neatly tucked in at the waist, her blouse had become completely unbuttoned.

"I work in the circus," Windrow said, tucking in his shirt. "I only have fun when I'm at home." He zipped his fly. "Now about that picture." He walked over to the cart and poured a short hit of Scotch.

She pouted. "Make me."

Windrow looked at her. What did he care if they found her old man? "What about your property settlement?" he said tentatively. She formed the words *Make me* with her wet lips, but did not say them aloud.

He stood over her. "Make me," she whispered breathlessly. Martin Windrow slapped her, not too hard, but firmly, with the palm of his hand; and before she could ask he backhanded her, harder than he'd intended, so that she was knocked off the couch and her breath escaped her in a little scream.

Jesus Christ, Windrow said to himself. He rubbed the back of his hand. Something dripped down onto the back of his thigh.

Honey Trimble picked herself up and meekly, in her stocking feet, padded to the bookcase. Windrow looked at his Scotch. He picked up Mrs. Trimble's drink and sniffed. It had no odor.

When Honey Trimble turned back to him, carrying a large scrapbook he was standing with his own drink looking at the view. She curled up on the couch with the book and waited.

"Just the picture, please," he said, "ma'am."

She put the book down rather loudly on the coffee table and began to thumb rapidly through it. She extracted a photograph from under its plastic and handed it to him.

It was a color picture of a pale man shackled to a wall. He was naked, spread-eagled, bound and gagged.

27

"I took that just before we separated," she said. Then she giggled.

The wall looked like masonry, and he thought he could make out the edge of a floor drain in the extreme foreground.

"Did you show this to the cops?"

"Oh, no. They weren't as nice as you. Besides"—she giggled again—"there were too many of them." More giggles. "I gave them the museum catalog, with pictures of the staff."

He extended the photograph back to her. "These Polaroids are pretty fuzzy," he said, "and there's a line or something across the mouth. Do you have anything else?" She swiped the photograph out of his hand. "The mouth is very important," he added, "for purposes of identification."

She flipped furiously through the scrapbook, backward, he noted, and extracted another snapshot. This time it was a black-and-white of the same man, but he was sitting on the same couch Honey Trimble was sitting on, fully clothed, holding a drink and looking at the photographer's feet. On the table behind the couch stood glasses and bottles, all of them various degrees of empty, and among them Windrow could make out a corner of the very photo album Mrs. Trimble now held open in her lap. The man looked moody, distracted, and slightly unhappy. Possibly he was uncomfortable or bored. The picture window behind him was lit up by the camera flash. There were arms and shoulders on both sides of the shot, obviously taken during a party, but no other faces were visible.

Windrow slipped the picture into his coat pocket and set his drink on the wheeled tray. "Thank you, Mrs. Trimble," he nodded and headed for the front door. Mrs. Trimble petulantly, but almost menacingly, slammed the scrapbook closed and stood up to follow him.

One foot across the threshold, Windrow turned to look at her. "By the way, Mrs. Trimble . . ."

She looked at him, all eyes. "Yes?"

"How well did your husband, your ex-husband, know Virginia Sarapath?"

Mrs. Trimble draped herself around her front door. "Well,

I'm sure I don't know, but I *assume* they were sleeping together."

"Oh? Why?"

"Why? Well, people just *do*, don't they? Sleep together?" She veiled her eyes. "Well! *Some* people do . . ."

"Right. Good night, Mrs. Trimble . . ." He turned away. "By the way"—he turned back again—"who's your master?"

She looked at him. Except for the fact that he wasn't buying, it was as if she thought she was the snake and he was the frog.

Then he thought he heard a door close, softly, somewhere behind her.

"It might have been you," she said. She blew a kiss at him and slammed the door.

Chapter Six

From the passenger seat of his old Toyota, Windrow could watch the front door of Honey Trimble's house. It was a shingled, cut-up affair, the shingles long since turned black in the weather. Once he saw a light go on in an upstairs room.

Outside, the fog thickened. Windrow sat with his pint of stakeout brandy in his lap and listened to the foghorns on the bay. Beyond the Trimble house, much higher up, he could see the red glow from the Sutro Tower, its individual lights diffused by the dense fog.

So someone had listened in on their conversation; probably had witnessed the attempted rape. He ran the scene backward and forward in his mind. The scene had been lurid enough to be compromising; had photos been taken? Compromising, that is, to a man who had a reputation to look after. Windrow didn't have that problem. If anybody had anything to lose, it was Mrs. Trimble. If a picture of that scene were to get out, what would the neighbors think? Nothing, that's what they would think. This is the

29

Wild West, where men can be anything and women do whatever they want to do.

Windrow permitted himself a mirthless laugh and sipped his pint. His mind began to wander, and his eyes flitted up and down the block, looking for nothing in particular. He looked at his watch: 10:30. This is much worse than being a cop, he thought, much worse. He hunched down in the seat, and flicked on the radio. If he left it on long enough, it would run the battery down. Nice thing about San Francisco, though, there are lots of hills. Could always release the brake, turn on the key, and let her roll. She'd start in fifty feet, or a half block.

He thought of the last high-speed chase he'd had, as a policeman. The guy he was chasing was a good driver with an excellent car, and Windrow couldn't keep up with him. Finally, trying too hard, Windrow had sideswiped eleven cars parked on both sides of the street. The police vehicle was completely destroyed, and Windrow wound up slumped over the wheel, laughing very contentedly. The good old days. Do that now it'd be jail, pure and simple. The Toyota wasn't even insured.

The light upstairs in Trimble's place went out. What did Windrow know about the hand that turned out that light? Did it belong to Honey Trimble? Or to Herbert? Had it been Herbert there in the house, listening? Or someone else? It didn't seem likely that Honey Trimble's "master," as she'd called him— her?—would be her ex-husband. Who, then? It was more in line with an ex-wife's behavior toward an ex-husband that she'd tried to get Windrow to leave with a Polaroid of her ex in bondage. Or maybe she was just crazy. Definitely, he decided, taking a small sip of the brandy, she wasn't normal.

He put the bottle into the glove compartment. And those bruises. Who did her that favor? For, undoubtedly, they had been a favor. Was she, even now, running her fingernail over the new bruises he'd almost certainly left on her mouth? He wiggled the little finger of his right hand. He could still feel the sting of the two unintentionally hard slaps he'd given her. How had she provoked that?

Easy. I'm working for the firm that's working for her. She can make me do anything she wants, as long as I take the money.

The man with the answers.

Anything?

A rectangle of yellow light opened up in the side of the Trimble house. Through the fog, Windrow saw two figures gesture at each other. One came away from the house; the other, the silhouette of Honey Trimble, retreated. The first figure walked, unhurriedly, up the hill, toward Windrow's badly parked Toyota, using a cane. It was a man. As he passed the Toyota, Windrow slid under the wheel and opened the driver's door. The dome light illuminated the man's startled face. It was the face of the man in the two photographs.

Windrow stood up on the sidewalk, leaving the door open. As he did so, the fog surged through the dark trees over their heads, and their leaves hissed and rattled. The man shivered visibly.

"Mr. Trimble? Herbert Trimble?"

"What—Oh." Apparently the man recognized Windrow, for when he saw his face, he smiled, as if the two of them shared a secret. "Mr. Windrow, I presume, though we've never met."

"I guess that now you're going to make some crack about common ground."

The man sniggered. "No, no. Not at all. What takes place on the premises of the former Mrs. Trimble is certainly no concern of mine."

"Oh, yeah? What exactly has been taking place, Mr. Trimble?"

"Oh, my friend . . ." the man said, looking both ways, up and down the sidewalk. He leaned closer to Windrow; Windrow found himself leaning imperceptibly away. "She sponsors the most incredible, ah, *sexual events* . . . ." He laughed. "You haven't heard?"

"I don't get around much."

"Perhaps you'd be at home in a slighty, ahm, lower neighborhood."

31

"You certainly have a way with the words, Mr. Trimble," Windrow said, reaching into his coat pocket.

"Well, I am a writer, Mr. Windrow."

"Right. Well, then you can probably read, too, huh, Mr. Trimble. It's my current mission to present you with these papers, concerning certain legalities involving your divorce."

"Why, thank you."

"Though, personally, I don't see why you couldn't have worked this out with the lady face to face, and saved yourself a bunch of money. Lawyers, errand boys . . . we all have little meters on us."

"Yes, yes, I quite understand, and you're quite right, we do get along famously; but, really, the poor bitch wants absolutely everything."

It was true that Trimble's way of putting all possible intonation on every second or third word he said was annoying enough, and that most of what the man said had a distinctly false ring to it, as if his exaggerated manner of speech was an act, employed merely to throw Windrow off the track of the smallest grain of truth. But Windrow had a less specific and more insidious feeling, akin to the one that occasionally rose in his sternum to indicate the scene or aura of nasty events, a vague stirring just below his conscious awareness that he was being completely had, but didn't understand how. He saw that, though it was dark on this street, Trimble, too, felt Windrow's growing awareness, but made no attempt to distract or staunch it. Rather, he continued with his mincing calumnies about his wife while, behind them, he waited for Windrow to make some kind of move.

Windrow changed the subject.

"Did you murder the Sarapath girl, your neighbor, Mr. Trimble?"

The man called Trimble allowed his face to be overwhelmed by a huge and, Windrow thought, demonically amused grin, but said nothing.

"Well, Mr. Trimble?"

The man composed his features and said, "Really, Mr.

Windrow, I won't even countenance that kind of suggestion. I hardly—in fact, I didn't know her at all."

"So?"

The man looked at Windrow a bit more intently. "What do you mean, *so?* One would like to get personally *involved* with the people whom one murders, get to *know* them a little before the ax falls, wouldn't one?"

Windrow allowed as how he imagined one would.

"Yes," the man said, nodding his head almost as if to himself. "Yes."

Windrow took a shot in the dark. "But tell me, Mr. Trimble. How did you know about the ax?"

Trimble's eyes narrowed. "Ax? What ax . . . ? Oh, the ax! Oh, come, come, Mr. Windrow, that's merely a figure of speech. You know that. I may just as well have said—er, the, uh—the whip, the whip, yes. Before the whip comes down." The man cackled. "You see," he added.

"I see that the police are wanting to talk to you, Mr. Trimble, about the Sarapath girl."

"Well, I imagine they'll find me when they need me."

"You want to leave me your number, so's I might pass it on?"

The man was looking up the sidewalk. "I'm in the book," he said.

"But you're not in my book, Herbert." Windrow moved to face him. "Don't you want to be in my book?" He heard the tang of steel, a swish, and saw a long gleam in the man's hand. A sword cane, Windrow thought. I don't believe it. The point shimmered a few inches from his throat.

"Could be the last page of your diary, gumshoe," the man hissed. "Get back in the car."

"Look, Zorro . . ."

"*Get back in the car!*"

Windrow got back in the car.

"Close the door."

Windrow closed the door.

"Now beat it."

He turned the key. After a few sluggish groans, the motor

33

caught. The Toyota took a few rounds of jacking back and forth to get out, but the unsheathed threat assured the process. Windrow let the Toyota coast down the hill and around the corner; he watched his rearview mirror until the shadowy figure backing up the sidewalk turned out of the glass. He killed the motor and the lights and coasted into a driveway.

He lay down on the seat. Soon a small car came around the corner, very fast.

Windrow started the Toyota, backed out, and followed the two red taillights.

Chapter Seven

An old transistor radio on top of a stack of paperback books played tunes from the forties quietly.

Marilyn Sarapath wrung the washcloth over the bathroom sink, rinsed it, and wrung it out again. She emptied the bowl of pink-tinged water and refilled it with fresh, cold water. She took a bottle of peroxide and another of iodine out of the medicine cabinet. With the practiced artifice of an experienced waitress, she gathered these things into her arms—the bowl perched on the leveled thumb and forefinger, which pinched the twisted cloth, the necks of the two bottles caught between the lower fingers of her right hand, a dry cloth draped over her wrist. Carrying her drink in her left hand, she walked into her bedroom. She placed her articles of first aid on the cluttered nightstand next to the bed and, taking a drink, surveyed the prostrate form on her bed.

It was the form of a man with no clothes on, lying on his stomach. Between his stomach and the bedclothes a white towel interceded, catching the slow trickle of blood, now virtually ceased, from the wound in the left buttock. Black, ugly thread ends stuck up from the recent tear, like the legs of an upturned centipede; but Marilyn didn't let this startling sight distract her from a proper appraisal of the rest of the torso: white, well muscled, thinking about going soft, slightly hairy. Nice legs, too. Only the neck showed signs of having recently seen the sun; the rest of the body was smooth and pale. She'd seen the scars, new and old, and the slight paunch, not quite overhanging the fresh wound in front; she'd heard the sharp intake of breath as he'd rolled over. On the whole, she'd reflected, it was just as well he'd turned the other way, face down, though her eyes drifted curiously to the dark hair, high up, between his legs. This side looked like it had seen slightly less action than the front.

The front side, propped on its elbows, extended itself far enough toward the side of the bed to hang up the telephone, then, turning its face sideways, lay itself down on the pillows and closed its eyes.

"Ready?" she said.

"Ready."

"Have a drink first," she counseled.

"You have one."

"I just did."

"Have another."

"Thanks." She took a big slug from her glass and set it down on the night table. She sat on the edge of the bed and pressed the wound with the washcloth.

"Mmmm," said Martin Windrow.

"I'll bet." Marilyn dipped the washcloth in the basin and gently blotted the fresh blood as it welled out of the wound.

"Well, something's going on," Windrow said sleepily.

Marilyn rinsed the washcloth, wrung it out thoroughly, and poured hydrogen peroxide directly into the wound. The stuff foamed up out of it and ran down both sides of the thigh. She dabbed at the runoff with the washcloth.

"So," she said, "the detective sits in his car, down the street from the suspect's house, for half an hour after he'd said goodnight. He is said to be staking the place out." She squeezed more peroxide into the cut, and dabbed at the runoff. "A man comes out of her house, walks past the dick's car. He stops long enough to threaten the dick with a"—she giggled—"a sword cane. Intimidated, the dick leaves. D'Artagnan, he gets into another car, two shorts up the block." She put the washcloth in the basin and picked up a spool of thread and a needle from the night table. "You sure you want me to do this?"

"Positive. Think of the money I'll save."

"Think it'll cover the price of a new ass?"

Windrow opened one eye and winked at her. "How much for a used one?"

She jabbed his good buttock with the needle. A little dot of blood appeared. Windrow said nothing and smiled up at her.

"I saw your jaw twitch."

"Impossible," Windrow said, closing his eyes again.

"Next time it'll be right in that gash, tough guy, and we'll see what happens."

"Don't forget to twist it."

She stuck out her tongue, squinted, and tried to thread the needle. "Back on the television, the dick tails a late-model Buick to an address in Hayes Valley, to a block where it is so dark the dick can't get a make on the john, or the house number."

"Different racket."

"Hm?"

"Different racket. Guy's not a john, he's a subject."

"Subject? What're you, an artist?"

"Subject, subjection, subject."

"Got it. Ready?"

"I thought you were almost finished."

"I haven't even started yet!"

"Oh. Did you cook the point?"

"Ha? Whazzat? You want another bowl of argot?"

"The needle. You gotta flame up the needle, for the germs."

"Oh, right! Germs! Guy's got a new hole in his ass, from a straight razor some child pornographer pulled out of his shoe, and he's worried about germs on a nice girl's needle."

"I might get hepatitis. An aneurysm."

She retrieved a cigarette out of a pack on the night table, and a lighter. She lit the cigarette and, squinting through the smoke, held the gas flame under the needle, which glowed red almost immediately.

"Matter of fact," she said pensively, watching the flame, "I've had done with all that . . . ouch."

"What do you mean, 'ouch'? I'm the patient."

"Listen, gumshoe. *You* were supposed to come over here to help *me* through the whirlies."

"Nothing like occupying the hands to take the mind off one's problems."

"Look, are you sure—"

"Do it."

She took a long drag off her cigarette, propped it in an ashtray on the nightstand. She caught the bulge of flesh along the inside of the buttock, between her thumb and her fingers, and did it. Two neat sutures on one end of the knife wound, to replace the two that had torn out when Honey Trimble pushed Windrow onto her sofa. She tied each with two square knots, not too tight. Martin Windrow didn't say a word. Marilyn cut a large piece of gauze from a roll and doubled it over several times to make a thick pad and soaked it in iodine. This she placed over the sutures, pressing it a little to squeeze the disinfectant into the wound. Over this piece of gauze she placed a gauze pad with a plastic backing and secured the whole bandage with several pieces of tape. When she'd finished, Marilyn said nothing, but pressing the tape ends into place around and over the wound, she let the palm and fingers and fingers of her free hand brush up and down the small of Windrow's back. She flared the motion up under his shoulder blades and gently back down the side of his rib cage, and repeated it. Still, with her other hand, she fussed slowly about the dressed wound.

"So the detective calls the cops," she said softly, with pauses between her phrases, "and gives the location as being the hideout of one Herbert Trimble." She was using both hands now. They slid up Windrow's spine and grasped the thick muscles behind his shoulders and neck and kneaded them.

"Really," Windrow said into the pillows.

Her hands sculpted his hips. "Ahhhh," she said, exhaling. "Medicine's a demanding profession." Her thumbs traced the lines where his buttocks met his thighs.

"So why—" Windrow said, one hand scratching an eyebrow, "why did Honey Trimble give the detective a picture of a man hiding in her house? A little higher. Is she afraid of her husband? Was it a veiled call for help? Was that man her husband?"

"Not necessarily," she said. "But he was the man in the photograph the detective had in his pocket when he left Mrs. Trimble's.

"Subsequently, the detective, after waiting a decent amount of time, called police headquarters and spoke to a friend. Who was the man to whom an anonymous tipster had led them?

" 'None of your goddamn business,' the detective was told. Hmmm."

"So he called another friend downtown. Court reporter. Had homicide just brought in one Herbert Trimble? And if so, on what charges had they booked him? Ahhhh.

" 'Who? Herbert Trimble? Never heard of him,' the reporter says.

" 'Ah so,' says the clever dick, stumped. 'So, Charlie, what's new downtown?'

" 'Well,' says Charlie, 'they just brought in a guy on *suspicion* of being Herbert Trimble. Turned out he wasn't.'

" 'Ah, yes. The endless hours of fruitless police work. So the guy looked like him, eh?'

" 'Not at all,' says the newspaper man, obviously relishing the detective's fishing expedition. 'He looks like some guy called Harry . . .'

"He looks like some guy called Harry—Harry . . ." She tugged gently at Windrow's shoulder.

"Harry Feyn," said Windrow, rolling over.

"The editor of, of . . ." she was losing the thread of the story. She was staring at him.

"*Brandish*," he said.

"The magazine of—oh, my God," she whispered, smiling.

His eyes followed her gaze to its focus. Her hands met them there.

"Mine, too," he said with a grin.

38

Chapter Eight

The air wasn't too thick, though it was thick enough, and the stairs weren't too steep, though there were two flights of them; but Martin Windrow climbed them slowly, and when he'd gotten to the top of them, he breathed heavily.

It's a good thing I don't smoke, he thought to himself as he limped down the hall, his breath rasping slightly through the mucous in his throat. Then again, because he didn't smoke, he could smell the pungency of iodine that wafted around him when he stopped. He could smell the stale whiskey on his breath. And he could smell and still taste someone else's day and night and early-morning cigarettes in his mouth. And, yes, among these odors he could pick out others: Someone's cat had sprayed the corner where the hall wall met the stairhead. He could smell cops as he approached the end of the hallway that led to the opposing doors of Virginia Sarapath and Herbert Trimble. And he could smell . . . a perfume, one he'd smelled before.

There was a new padlock on Virginia's door and a straight-backed chair in front of it. Under the chair were two editions of the *Examiner,* and three or four empty Styrofoam cups. Someone had run out of coffee, and the morning *Chronicle* had been on the street for an hour.

Windrow stood between the two apartments and stared at the knob on Herbert Trimble's door, counting the stitches in his mouth with his tongue. The blood was the same type as the Sarapath girl's, Windrow thought, and it was on the inside of the door. Who knows, it might have been Trimble. He'd always wanted to skin a woman, probably his ex-wife. But he was some kind of writer, a hack writer; he wrote hack horror stories for a cheap pulp magazine under a pseudonym. Didn't that mean he got to take out his aggressions against women on paper? Wouldn't that be sufficient revenge for their transgressions, real or imagined, for a man who lived mainly in his imagination?

The long, lugubrious sound of a cello, its lowest note carefully bowed, penetrated the door as Windrow stared at it. He couldn't believe his ears. Short strokes on the same string reinforced his original impression: Someone was in Herbert Trimble's apartment, tuning a cello. As Windrow listened, the musician successively bowed and tuned the rest of the strings and then, after a pause, began to play scales and exercises. Slowly at first, then faster and faster, with precision.

Windrow looked at the empty chair, its back against Virginia Sarapath's door. So the uniformed cop played the cello?

Very carefully, he tried the door. The knob turned easily and quietly. Still standing in the hall, he eased the door open with his fingertips. The air of the room as it moved to meet him bore the unmistakable odor of burning marijuana. The scales didn't stop, but now little scraps of musical compositions began to appear in them. The cellist played a scale up in major, then down in minor that modulated into another major, then up in that major, then down again using a piece of actual music that went in the same direction. Then he modulated out of that piece. When he got back down to the next note in his progression he left the musical piece and, modulating, turned upward again in a scale or through another musical piece. The whole exercise had impressive, virtuosic coherence. Windrow closed the door and stood in the entryway, listening. The player was good; and stoned, too, judging by the thick air in the apartment.

He walked into the studio. The man sitting in the simple folding metal chair, facing a lyre-shaped stand heaped with music, sawing and swaying with a look of furious concentration, took no heed of him. Though hunched in that position peculiar to cellists at work, the man looked to be of medium height, with blond, almost platinum hair. Windrow noticed immediately that the man's hair was the same color as Mrs. Trimble's, only much shorter. He wore sneakers, a pair of lemon-yellow pressed pants, a pin-striped shirt with cigarette pocket and button-down collar, a French-style cravat, and some kind of bracelet. Perspiration ran in two rivulets from his left sideburn to his jaw-bone, and as he worked at his cello, the sweat gleamed in the morning light.

The room was more disheveled than it had been the previous day. The Murphy bed was still down out of the wall closet, the same closet in which, only yesterday, Steve Gleason had found Trimble's drugs.

Obviously, Trimble had more than one stash.

The bed sheets were extremely rumpled and creased; they looked like they hadn't been laundered in a couple of weeks. Most of the blanket draped to the floor, on which a number of articles of clothing were scattered. Among them something gleamed, catching Windrow's eye. He studied it, and its shape became apparent to him, and then he recognized it. It was the necklace Mrs. Trimble had worn the night before, when he'd seen her at her house. The big, square links, connected by the little steel annulets were unmistakable. It was possible, just possible, that it was a duplicate . . .

Mentally, Windrow shrugged. Some people could never get themselves straight over a divorce. They would fling themselves away from their partners, hire lawyers, sue and threaten each other, then, after weeks of animosity, take off with their estranged spouse for three days in honeymoon hotel in Carmel. Though, he reflected, a bed's a bed.

Then he realized that the rest of the links in the outlandish necklace, invisible to him, were hidden in the folds of a black material very similar to that of the pants he'd last seen Mrs. Trimble wearing. He looked behind him toward the bathroom door situated directly across from the hall entrance. It was closed. So they weren't alone, he and the cellist. Turning slightly, so that he could keep a corner of his eye on the closed door, he cleared his throat, loudly.

"Ahem. Mr. Trimble?"

The man glanced up at Windrow, finished the scale he was on, and stopped playing. He appeared to be seriously considering the answer to this question, but something else, another question, perhaps, flitted behind his eyes.

"Yes?"

"You're Herbert Trimble?"

"Yes."

"I've got some papers for you." Windrow reached into his pocket and pulled out the copies he'd gotten from Emmy, after he'd left Marilyn.

"You should hire a telepath," she'd said, "or a psychic. People could give you the runaround."

"They work for free, too?" was all Windrow could manage as he'd headed for the door. Now he handed the two pages to the man he hoped, finally, was Herbert Trimble. Trimble glanced at them, smiled, and stuck them between the pages of a music book on the stand.

"What's so funny?" said Windrow. "How come everybody's getting a little kick out of this lousy court order?"

"Who, you mean all two of us?" said Trimble.

"I'm not laughing," said Windrow. "Where were you two nights ago, about two thirty in the morning?"

The man stroked four melodramatic bass notes on his instrument and watched Windrow, his eyes not blinking. They were the famous clichéd notes of the theme to *Dragnet*, one of the original T.V. cop shows. The guy knows something, Windrow thought, though I'm no iridologist.

"Right here, trying to get some sleep," Trimble said irritably. "Only that bitch next door was working her way through Masters and Johnson, backwards, and I couldn't close my eyes for the visions." He bowed the low string again, then rounded his stroke, so as to let the bowing catch some of the other strings, and fretted a little progression. "As of dancing sugar plums," he said, "with nylon legs."

"Why should that bother you, Trimble? Had it never happened before?"

"Never," said Trimble. He looked Windrow in the eye. Trimble's eyes were big and wet. "Anywhere," he almost whispered that one, as if its certainty were as horrible as its truth.

"What? Never? Anywhere? How did you know that?"

"Oh," said Trimble, thumbing through some music on the stand, "I get around."

"I know," said Windrow. "I met your wife yesterday."

Trimble turned to look at him. But his face didn't show shock or outrage at the deliberate crudity of Windrow's remark, merely amusement. Trimble chuckled. "*Ex*," he said. "*Ex*-wife." He laughed out loud. Something was tickling him, no doubt about it. But no sooner had he shown his amusement to Windrow than he frowned and looked away. He stared at the baseboard on the other side of the cello for a moment. As if coming to himself, he looked up at the music, thought a moment, and rapidly thumbed through it.

"You've heard of Elgar?" he said, nervously arranging the pages of the book so that they might stay open without help. Windrow reached over and closed the book.

"Yeah, yeah. So your wife has read the Kama Sutra, how come the lady next door bothered you so much? Was it loud?"

Herbert Trimble stared at the cover of the book. "Very loud," he said. "She kept me up all night."

"All night?"

"All night, until about four o'clock or so. Then, then I— well I . . ."

"Come on, Herbert. Spit it out. It's time."

"I had this idea for a story. I, you see, I write these silly things . . . Hack them I mean, for money." He ran his hand up and down the back of the neck of his cello, lovingly. "She's an expensive habit," he said dreamily. "Time, you know. It takes an awful lot of time to make this whore play."

"So you got up and started to write this story."

"Yes. I'd had the first line for hours, the idea, the whole story even, I guess. . . . But it's so degrading to let the libido run around undisciplined like that. And it takes energy, precious energy."

"Away from her?" Windrow indicated the cello.

Trimble smiled and glanced shyly at Windrow. "Yes, you—perhaps you understand. It takes time, and energy,

43

just like she takes time and energy, but the difference is a matter of worlds."

"Her," Windrow said.

"Oh, yes," said Trimble, "I'm not unique in that. Ask any musician. His instrument is his animas, his *her* . . . Of course," he added, pointing to his desk with his bow, "there's always *her*, too."

Windrow looked at the manuscript stacked neatly on one corner of the desk behind Trimble. "You mean *The Art of Death*?"

"Yes, Mr. Windrow." Trimble batted his eyelids. "I'm a bigamist." He laughed gaily. "There are lots of *hers* in my life, Mr. Windrow, as you are beginning to see." He laughed and bowed a few carefree notes.

"Yes, it looks that way, Mr. Trimble. What about the one next door?"

Trimble looked at Windrow, frowned, then shifted his glance back to the music stand. He bit his lip.

"I typed the first line," he said. He looked down at his bow and minutely adjusted the knob that tightened the horsehairs. "Then the tone of her voice, which I'd been listening to for hours at that point, the tone of her voice . . . changed."

Windrow waited "Changed how, Mr. Trimble?"

"Until then, her moans and exclamations had been mostly of pleasure—some of them, perhaps quite a few of them, emanated from those little pains one encounters on the way to greater pleasures, but everything I'd heard seemed to derive from . . . well, from good sportsmanship, shall we say. And, therefore, it was none of my business."

"But something changed that."

"Not something, Mr. Windrow. Someone. Someone began to do things differently. Someone had begun to hurt the lady Sarapath."

"What did you hear? Blows? A shot? Screams?"

"Oh, no, no. It was very subtle, at first. In fact, it had probably been going on for some time before I noticed it. But notice it I did. The woman was experiencing pain. Very complicated, profound pain."

44

"Complicated? Profound? You mean it was emotional as well as physical?"

"Yes, but more than that. She was emotionally involved with it, true, but she must have been experiencing something that was new to her, something that surprised her, perhaps shocked her, but somehow it, the pain, was . . . *seducing* her. She couldn't run away from it, she couldn't turn it off, she couldn't stop it."

"Couldn't?"

"Wouldn't."

"Why? Why not?"

"Because, Mr. Windrow, she was enjoying it."

Trimble had been applying resin to his cello bow. He stopped and looked at Windrow, who stared back at him.

"It was excruciating, Mr. Windrow, for me to sit there and listen to it, but—I will be perfectly frank with you—it was also . . . titillating. I hope you don't misunderstand me."

There was a pause.

"So you continued to write?" Windrow finally asked, quietly.

"I never got past the first line. By the time I'd brought myself to write that, the disturbance next door was becoming more than I could bear. Once again, sitting behind my desk, I sat and listened. I listened for a long time." Trimble suddenly began to fidget. The end of the bow bobbed up and down below the music stand. "Until I heard one last long, sobbing, excruciating, broken . . ." He turned the palms of his hands upward. The bow end flicked upward and tapped the underside of the music stand in response to his loss of words. ". . . moan," he said. "It was the hideous, hopeless moan of someone completely, thoroughly, utterly lost. A cry of the damned."

Windrow waited for a moment. He didn't think that Trimble needed any prompting, but when no further information seemed forthcoming, he said, "Was that when you went next door, Mr. Trimble?"

Trimble looked at him briefly and looked away. He'd begun to shake, just perceptibly. His head was rigid, at a peculiar angle to his neck. His eyes stared helplessly at some scene reenacting itself in the dust and shadows under the bed.

"I went next door," he managed to say, apparently with great effort. Windrow thought that the man's voice was beginning to change on account of the strain.

"You went next door . . ."

Trimble looked up into Windrow's eyes. Trimble's eyes were sad, afraid, resigned, faraway, and . . . Windrow realized—too late—that Trimble's eyes saw someone else. Whoever that someone else was had great agility, too, for before Windrow could turn around and see who it was, the someone had, as they say, jerked the rug out from under Windrow, and turned out the lights. And the agile someone was generous. In the darkness that followed, the someone made a present to Windrow. It was a beautiful display of sparks, brightly colored, and they were wonderful sparks. He thought that he could feel them, behind his eyes, better than he could see them, just before he could neither feel nor see anything at all.

Chapter Nine

Martin Windrow tested his eyes and saw the large, squinting, purple face of Max Bdeniowitz, inches from his own. He closed his eyes and tried to think of naked women, but all he got were people in overcoats on flat, overcast beaches. He turned his head from one side to another and smacked his lips. The inside of his mouth tasted like the floor of a dairy shed; and his tongue seemed three sizes too large. And the pain. When he moved his head, his skull creaked like a dilapidated piece of wooden furniture. His eyes had been removed and batted around and put back out of round, in the wrong sockets. The fingers of his left hand pinched tenuously for the slightest purchase on the bare wooden floor beneath him.

He forced his eyelids to become slits. They allowed only the minimum of optical information to pass through them.

What he saw was more than enough, and he groaned. Above him was a circle of human figures, all of them cops. Only one of the figures was paying any attention to him, but if he'd had his choice, he'd rather that all of them were watching him grovel on the floor, instead of the single one who was now glowering down at him.

A patient man Max Bdeniowitz wasn't. If Max had a man on stakeout, he'd rather that man do enticing body language to attract the subject he was waiting for, than just sit in his car and drink coffee, waiting. If a man held hostages in a building at gunpoint, with plastic explosives wired to himself and the Transamerica Pyramid, Max would not be the man to call in to negotiate. If Max somehow by mistake showed up on the scene, he would go in after the guy, while everybody else helped evacuate the neighborhood, to take the maniac's toys away from him. If the guy's arm came off with the gun, too bad. It would still be attached to the gun, too, when it showed up in court as evidence. Max was an honest cop.

And right now, Max was impatient. He prodded Windrow's ribs with his toe.

"Wake up, Marty. Show-and-tell time."

"Ow," said Windrow, wincing. "Kick a good one."

"If there was a good one left, I'd kick it, Windrow. Get up."

Windrow crawled to a wall and sat himself up against it. As he lifted his head, an avalanche occurred inside it, and miscellaneous retired brain matter cascaded into his neck.

"What happened?"

"Sorry, Windrow. That's my question. Just tell us what happened, and then one of the boys will give you a nice ride downtown."

"Downtown? Why? It's not my bowling night."

"If I got anything to do with it, Windrow, you'll never bowl again. What happened?"

Windrow had no idea what had happened. He couldn't remember anything since yesterday. He fought a wave of dizziness, then his stomach turned over. He groaned.

Silence.

"Look, Max . . ."

"I am. It's making me sick."

"Suppose you tell me where we are first."

"Oh, come on, Windrow . . ."

"Just a hint, Max."

"Look, Windrow, if there wasn't the press outside, I'd fill you with booze and drown you in the bathtub—"

"Bathtub . . . There's a bathtub here . . .?"

Bdeniowitz sighed. "Yeah, but you can't afford the rent."

"The bathroom. She must have come out of the bathroom."

Bdeniowitz looked significantly at Steve Gleason, who sat on the Murphy bed, his hands in the pockets of his trenchcoat, smoking a cigarette. "She?" he said.

"His wife, Mrs. Trimble. She must have slipped out of the bathroom and coldcocked me while he was telling me his story."

"He, Windrow?"

"Trimble. Herbert Trimble."

Bdeniowitz wiped a hand over his face. "Sweet Heysoos," he breathed. "So it was Trimble."

"Yeah," said Windrow, "it was Trimble. He was sitting right behind you, playing the cello."

"Fruitcakes, alla them," Gleason said around his cigarette.

"The cello," Bdeniowitz repeated tonelessly. He looked behind him. The music stand was there, and the chair, but no cello. "What cello?"

Gleason shook his head. "It's not here, Max."

Bdeniowitz scowled. "You trying to tell me we got a guy here, a fugitive from murder one, who sneaks back to the scene of the crime, with a stakeout on it yet, to play the cello? And then he steals it?"

Gleason shook his head sadly. "Fruitcakes."

"That's what he was doing, Max. I didn't know from anything, just came back here to get a look at things, see what I might turn up."

Bdeniowitz scowled even more. "And how the hell were you figuring to get back in one of these joints, Windrow?"

"I thought, you know, just a chance, but I thought that you might be here, Max, to unlock them for me." Windrow

48

looked up innocently. Gleason rolled his eyes. Max turned a color.

"It just so happens, you *private dick*," he said the words in a tone of utter contempt, "that we had this joint set up, on the chance that this kink might come home for his galoshes."

A little light bulb blinked on over Windrow's head. Everybody in the room could see it. "Oh, so that's how come the chair was empty, you told the uniform to go out for coffee, like, whistling all the way, every hour or so . . . huh?"

Bdeniowitz was trying to squeeze his cheeks and his nose and his eyes all into one point with one beefy hand.

"Yeah," said Gleason, suddenly animate. "And he goes, like, two and a half blocks to the drug store, cause they got the good coffee . . ."

"And there's a guy on the roof, across the way, who's on the lookout for Trimble . . ."

". . . in case he tries to slip back into his pad," Gleason finished the explanation with a flourish of his cigarette hand. "Bingo! We nab 'em."

"Say, that's great Max," said Windrow appreciatively. He put both his hands on the floor and pushed himself up. "I guess that means you got them on the way out, after they bashed me, and everything's tidied up." Everybody— Gleason, Bdeniowitz, and the two uniformed officers— looked at Windrow strangely. Windrow enumerated with his fingers: "I got the divorce notice delivered, and a headache for my troubles; you nabbed your prime murder-one suspect, and a nice bit in the papers. Smart police work." He brushed his hands together and looked around for his hat. "Great. Well, guess I'll be going."

Bdeniowitz said, "This what you're looking for?" and held up Windrow's hat.

"Oh, yeah. Thanks." But as he reached for it, Bdeniowitz dropped it on the floor.

"You're not going anywhere," Bdeniowitz said quietly, his eyes cold.

Windrow looked from Max to his men and back. One of their walkie-talkies squawked.

"What's the problem, Max?"

"We ain't got Trimble, we ain't got no dame, and we ain't got no suspects. All we got is you, apple."

"What? Me? What about you guys? What happened to your trap?"

"Johnson," said Bdeniowitz.

"Yeah."

"Tell."

"I returned from the decoy run to the drugstore at about ten thirty A.M. Been gone about half an hour. Resumed my seat and sat there for about fifteen minutes. Then I heard a noise, like a groan. I investigated. It came from this apartment. I tried the door. It was locked. I called Harry, across the street, on the two-way; he had the key. We drew our weapons, unlocked the door, and entered the apartment."

"And found what?"

Johnson indicated Windrow. "This," he said.

"Anyone else?"

"Nobody."

"Anything disturbed?"

"Hard to tell, sir."

"Thanks. Harry."

The other officer stepped forward.

"Have you seen Herbert Trimble enter or leave these premises today?"

"Nosir."

"Yesterday?"

"Nosir."

"How about the night guys?"

"Nobody's seen him, sir."

"Thanks." He looked at Windrow a moment, then said, "Well?"

"Well what?"

"Well, what are you doing standing there telling me you talked to Herbert Trimble this A.M.?"

"I did talk to him. He was sitting right there, playing the cello, when I came in."

"How did you get in?"

"Walked."

"The door was open?"

"Unlocked. I heard the cello, tried the door, found it unlocked, and walked in."

"And Trimble was here."

"And Trimble was here, Max."

"I think you ought to take a ride downtown."

"For what?"

"Oh, you know. Breaking and entering, interfering with police officers in their line of duty, withholding evidence . . ."

"Max, there were no cops here when I got here, and the door was open. Trimble was here, and he was playing the fucking cello."

"Why would—?"

"How would I know? He just was, that's all. I figured . . . I didn't figure anything. I figured I could give him his lousy papers and go home. And I did. And I would have. But then he starts telling me about the night of the murder."

Gleason looked up from the floor. Bdeniowitz didn't flinch. "Really," he said softly.

"Really. He said the girl spent the whole night over there moaning and groaning, like she was into heavy sex with someone, all night, he said."

Gleason looked at Bdeniowitz. Max continued to watch Windrow.

"He said he couldn't sleep all night, that he had an idea for a short story, hack work, you know, that's how he makes his money, since he quit the museum."

Bdeniowitz continued to say nothing.

"So he gets up to knock it out on the typewriter, about four o'clock, he said. And he's just written the first line, the one that you found on the machine, when something happened next door."

"What, what," said Bdeniowitz.

"I'm not sure, exactly. He said all the moans and groans changed tone."

"Tone?"

"Tone. They got—he said they began to sound more painful than pleasurable. So he stopped writing and tried

51

to figure out what to do about it. Finally, he went next door."

All the policemen had slowly moved closer to Windrow, the better to hear his story. After a pause, Gleason made an impatient gesture. "Whad happened, whad happened?"

Windrow shook his head and winced. "I don't know. That's when the lights went out."

Gleason stared at him in disbelief. Bdeniowitz allowed his right cheek a slight tic.

"I think I believe him," Windrow said. "I think he sat here, all right, trying to ignore whatever was going on on the other side of the wall, and that finally, for whatever reason, he forced himself to go over there and see what was up. And I think he saw something. I think he saw something that scared the hell out of him. But I don't think he killed her.

"In other words," Windrow continued, "I think he was a material witness, and the only one you've got. I think he got scared and ran. I think he went to his wife for help and that she is trying to help him. When I went by there last night to get a recent picture of him, she gave me the picture of Harry Feyn that led me to call you, to tip you to arrest him, thinking he was Trimble." Bdeniowitz raised his eyebrows and started to speak. "Well, how was I to know Max? I'd never seen the guy before. Whose picture did she give you?"

She tore a page out of a museum catalogue," Gleason volunteered, "and circled a face. His name was under it."

Well, I'll bet it's not him. She's helping him, I'm sure of it, and I think that guy Feyn is in on it. Did you get anything out of him?"

"He told us he hadn't seen Trimble."

"How about Mrs. Trimble?"

"They're friends. Better friends, it seems, since her hubby left."

"Why would he lead me to believe he was Trimble? Why did he take the papers I had for Trimble?"

"What papers?" said Bdeniowitz.

"The ones describing the disposition of their divorce

settlement. Didn't he have them on him when you arrested him?"

"We didn't see them."

"Well, I don't know how he fits in this, could just be a quick money angle, but Mrs T. is definitely trying to help Herbert out. I think he went to her with the story, and then they came back here. Maybe he came for his money, his dope, his galoshes, his cello lesson, I don't know. He looks and acts wigged-out enough to do anything."

"How about murder?" said Gleason, blowing smoke to one side.

"I don't know," said Windrow thoughtfully. "But I doubt it."

Bdeniowitz paced over to the window behind Trimble's desk and stared out of it, his hand in his pockets. Presently, he said, speaking to Windrow, "How do you know Mrs. Trimble was here? Did you see her?"

Windrow started to say yes, then thought about it.

"No," he said.

Bdeniowitz continued to look at the window. "Didn't see her, eh?"

Windrow fumbled, feeling foolish. "There was a necklace . . ."

"A necklace?"

"I saw it, right here on the floor. And a pair of pants."

"Yeah?"

"They were hers. She'd had them on when I saw her at her place, last night. I just assumed . . ." He stopped.

Bdeniowitz rocked on his heels in front of the window.

"Get out of here, apple," he said softly.

"But *somebody* hit me on the head while I was talking to Trimble. . . ."

"Get out of this building, get off this case, and don't leave town."

Windrow picked his hat up off the floor, where Bdeniowitz had dropped it.

" 'Don't leave town,' he says," Windrow grumbled, putting on his hat as Johnson opened the door. "On twenty-five dollars a week."

Chapter Ten

Windrow hit the street and walked. He didn't pay attention to a particular direction at first, but after a while he noticed the tall eucalyptus of the Panhandle a couple of blocks south and headed for them. Once in the middle of it, he followed the block-wide green strip as it paralleled the Haight-Ashbury. The fog that had blanketed the city the night before had retreated to Stanyan Street, and he could see the tall head of boiling white mists beyond, where the Panhandle suddenly widened into Golden Gate Park. Where Windrow walked the sun shone, and its light played minor rainbows at his feet in the ratcheting sprays of the sprinkler heads as he approached them. Here and there a nursemaid or young mother pushed a stroller with a little bundle of clothes in it, in which, if he looked closely, he could make out the central features of a little pink face. A raft of pigeons lifted off a sandy playground, circled a few feet over his head, and settled down behind him as he walked through them. Old men sat on the wooden benches, singly and in pairs, sipping beer from sacks or resting both hands on their canes. He passed one arthritic old fellow who looked as if he were shuffling as fast as he could go, and enthusiastically so, though he covered only a few inches at a step.

"Listen, sonny," the old fellow said, raising a finger at Windrow as he passed, and not slackening his pace. Windrow slowed and walked with him. "You got to do it in the morning, boy, first thing in the morning. If you work like a man all day and come home tired at night, why, you ain't in no kinda shape to make no kinda baby." The old geezer wagged his finger. "You just tell her to hold her horses and you save it, don't give in, turn over and you go right to sleep, son, and get a good night's rest. When you wake up in the morning you'll be fresh and new as a young boy.

54

And that's when you roll her over and, by God, you'll make a baby then, every time. And that's the truth." The old man put a hand on Windrow's arm and stopped, and Windrow did too. "Hang on a minute, son." He pulled a pint out of his back pocket. "I'm doin' pretty good, ain't I, keepin' up with you? For an old man?" He took a hit off his pint. "Care for a snort?" Windrow did, and had one. The whiskey going down added a new and familiar sensation to the two or so he'd already collected that day. He handed the bottle back and thanked the old man, who took another sip and capped it. He began shuffling again. Windrow took his leave. "Now, remember, sonny," the old man called after him, "git her in the *morning*, first thing. You'll always make a baby, that way." Windrow jaywalked across busy Oak Street and headed up Clayton, toward Haight. "And stay on top!" the old man shouted after him, gesturing with the bottle, "I got *eight grandchildren!*"

The clock read just after twelve, and it was dark and nearly empty and still a little stale from the night before, but the bar was open, and the woman behind the counter didn't mind at all serving a man a drink. Windrow had intended to ask for breakfast, but thinking the old man in the park had gotten him on to something, he ordered a whiskey and two aspirin. On the second sip he knew he'd made a mistake. He ordered a dark beer with an egg broken into it and headed for the bathrooms. Both doors were marked WOMEN, but he'd known that and opened the first one he came to.

He didn't have much to be sick with. He hadn't had a meal since breakfast in his office the night before. But the convulsions teased the broken rib and a few fresh, yellow sparks shot around in his vision. He tried not to make a mess of it, nor to make so much noise that he might embarrass himself. He'd always wanted to live a tidy, neat life, no trouble to anyone. But when the rib jabbed his stomach lining or the lung, he wanted to quit.

The sickness passed. He flushed the john and straightened up. His glottis and the nubs of gone tonsils were thick and swollen. The blood rushed from his head and left a wave of dizziness. He steadied himself, both hands on the sink. When the darkness passed, he opened his eyes and looked at the cry in the mirror.

He wet a paper towel under the sink spigot and swabbed gently at the blood dried in his eyebrow. It wasn't much of a cut, but it had bled a bit. He wasn't surprised Bdeniowitz hadn't pointed it out. Bdeniowitz would point out Windrow's obituary in the paper to him, in case he'd missed it, but in a small flesh wound he would take only passing pleasure. As he daubed at it, cleaning the hair, the little cut welled fresh blood, but soon clotted. He rinsed his mouth twice, pushed his hair back over the bump on his head, and went back to the bar.

On the countertop, next to his hat, stood a large glass of orange juice, a mug of steaming coffee, with cream, and a candle, lit. The bartender was nowhere to be seen. From the back room, beyond the end of the bar counter, came the sound of frying. The bartender came through the double doors with a plate of sourdough bread, sliced and buttered, and placed it in front of Windrow, to the left of the coffee. In between she carefully laid a napkin, with a fork on it and, properly spaced toward the coffee, a knife and spoon. The blade of the knife faced the empty center of the setting, where one might expect a plate full of food to turn up. Windrow looked at the little woman behind the counter. Her name was Connie, and she lived with the woman who owned this place. She was short and young, about twenty-five. She had very straight, light brown hair, cut in bangs in front so that it covered her ears and just touched her collar, no more. She had bright, clear, big gray eyes. She always looked intelligent and rarely spoke.

"Ah, Conrad," Windrow said. "What's this?"

"Your first meal," the little lady said, and she disappeared down the bar and into the galley.

Windrow looked at the trappings of real eating. He wasn't sure he knew what to do. He tested the orange juice. The glass had rivulets of coolness running down its outside, and ice cubes floated in the thick, pulpy juice. It was fresh-squeezed, and delicious, he thought. He finished the drink in two draughts.

Once he had lived with, and helped, a woman who was a friend of the woman who owned this bar, and the owner had never forgotten Windrow for it. Connie knew the story, and knew that Windrow was never to pay for what he drank in Orlando's. Today Connie had something extra, maybe just because she thought Windrow needed it, but more likely because he'd walked in looking like he could use help crossing the street.

Connie came back up the duck boards behind the bar with a large, steaming plate and placed it before Windrow. The plate contained two thick slices of ham, scrambled eggs, fried potatoes, a slice of orange, a little pile of preserves, and a sprig of parsley. The eggs and potatoes already had large grains of cracked pepper on them, and the ham had been sprinkled with salt. Windrow spread his arms and grinned.

"What, no catsup?" he said. Connie flashed her shy smile. While she went for the catsup, Windrow dug in with both hands. He thought he might be able to finish the meal before she got back with the catsup.

Over his third cup of coffee, Windrow asked Connie, "Heard from Elsa?"

Connie looked up briefly from the glass she'd been polishing, then went back to it.

"Dallas," she said.

Windrow looked at the front door, rubbed his stubble beard with a knuckle. Elsa.

"This coffee could use a little brandy in it, Conrad."

She topped off the cup with brandy and cream. Windrow sipped it.

Elsa was a whore. She was one of the expensive kind, which made her a prostitute. She was one of the really expensive kind, and that made her a call girl. Elsa was the lady who was the friend of the lady who lived with Connie and owned Orlando's, the one Windrow had helped out of a jam. He had helped her so much that he'd decided to hinder her a little bit, so he'd fallen in love with her. She claimed it was likewise, and they tried it out for a while. They lasted a year. One night, at the beginning of that year, to set an

57

example for the rest of it, they got a little drunk, and they smoked a little pot, and on the way home, all cuddly in the front seat, someone else jumped a red light and ran into them.

Nobody got hurt. But the other guy was much drunker than Windrow, and tried to punch Windrow out so he could tell the cops his side of the story first, without being interrupted. When the black-and-white got there, the drunk was stretched out in the fragments of his own headlights. Windrow had gotten so much satisfaction out of it, he'd forgotten all about the half-ounce of marijuana in his pocket. Everybody got a free ride downtown.

That's a pretty normal story for any night in the big city, but Martin Windrow had been a cop himself at the time, in homicide division. He worked for Bdeniowitz.

When they got downtown, everybody recognized everybody, except for the drunk, who was lonely and called his lawyer. When the police reporter heard the name of the lawyer, who was known to be very expensive, he sniffed out the name of the client. The drunk turned out to be a famous actor.

So the squad room was getting to be crowded by the time Bdeniowitz showed up. First he recognized Elsa, because he and Windrow had interrogated her twice the year before.

Hell, Windrow thought, a guy and girl have to meet somewhere, somehow.

Bdeniowitz hit the roof. He tried to cover for them for about an hour, then threw them to the wolves.

When the newspapers were finished, Windrow had lost his job, and the famous drunk was even more famous, though Windrow and Elsa got more ink.

They kept on living together. Windrow opened a little office and applied for his private ticket, but his first case was at home. All the publicity had attracted an old client of Elsa's, a rich, childlike psychopath from Los Angeles. He began to call daily.

He was always drunk, and he didn't want to talk to Windrow. He never bothered to realize that Windrow existed. He just wanted Elsa. Before it was over, Windrow had foiled a kidnapping and interrupted an attempt to throw acid in Elsa's face. It stopped when the playboy was murdered by his maid, who shot him with his own gun during a struggle in her bedroom, just as Windrow was buying a ticket to Los Angeles.

He and Elsa had lasted six months or so beyond that, then she was gone. She'd always worried about the potential threat her past posed to their future, but Windrow hadn't gone along with that—at first. After he'd lost his job and nearly been killed twice because of it, he wasn't too sure. And the peeping business was lousy. In that moment of weakness, when his faith wavered, she took off.

Dallas.

Don't leave town.

He snorted and sipped his coffee. Caffeine raced through his system, and alcohol. The two fought for the air in his blood, like two men fighting desperately over gold in a white-water raft, heading for the falls . . .

Chapter Eleven

Two women walked in the door and ordered two beers. One wore black leather, short hair, and chrome aviator's sunglasses. The other was slim, younger, wore short hair, tight jeans, and a western-cut blouse, unbuttoned nearly to the waist. Neither wore makeup. They took their beers to a shelf on the wall, near the pool table, and racked a game of nine ball. Windrow turned from the bar to watch them shoot.

The older woman ran five balls and scratched. The table was an older one, with smooth, level, felt-covered slate, mahogany rails, and woven leather pouches under each pocket so a scratch could be treated as such. She pulled a ball, spotted it, and rolled the cue down table to her partner. The younger girl sank three balls and masséd the cue ball into the kitchen. Her friend leaned on her cue and sipped beer. There wasn't a sign to that effect, but Windrow knew that only women were allowed to shoot pool in this bar. Men were tolerated at the counter, whether they drank or not, so long as they didn't bother the clientele.

Windrow had turned back to the bar and ordered whiskey with a beer chaser and two aspirin when Hanfield Braddock III walked in the front door.

Now, here was a character Windrow knew and liked and even admired a little bit. Hanfield Braddock III liked to say, loudly, that he was as queer as a two-dollar bill. In his mind, this afforded him the benefit of a pat cliché that made his sexual status perfectly clear to almost anybody who might be wondering, and at the same time imparted quasi-legitimacy to this status by virtue of the recent reissue of that denomination of currency. He referred to this irony as "fiduciary solvency," or "wet money," or a "cheap trick." He wrote a regular column for an established gay newspaper, the *Bat*, of which he was an original founder. As usual with all of Braddock's speech, this title had more than one meaning, but the main thrust of the editorial pages was radical advocacy, be it sexual, social, political, or otherwise. Braddock was an activist. He sat on the boards of foundations, committees, and small business enterprises. He knew the inside worlds of San Francisco politics and gay nightlife as well as anybody in the city. He knew powerful businessmen and politicians, pimps and lawyers, barflies and ballet stars. He liked to say they all had one thing in common: Somewhere along the line, they'd each gotten bored with the missionary position.

He waved hello to the two women playing pool and sat down next to Windrow. Calling Connie by name, he ordered a Calistoga and lime for himself and a double Screwing Gumshoe for Windrow, slapping him on the back and taking in his condition at a glance.

"Say, Marty," he said, looking over the wire rims of his glasses at the back of Windrow's head, "looks like you need a good phrenologist. Whad you do, answer an ad in the back of *Bat*?" Braddock giggled.

Windrow was sullen. "Think your phrenologist might tell me who gave me the new bump?"

"No," he said, "but he'll tell you what a good lay I am and give you my phone number."

"Yeah? Does he pay me or do I pay him?"

Braddock winked and massaged Windrow's neck. He hadn't taken his hand away since he'd slapped Windrow's back. "I'll pay both of you," he said huskily. "What do you say, huh, Marty? It's early. I haven't had mine yet today."

Windrow squinted through his headache at Braddock's reflection in the mirror. "Well, Hand, it's nice to be an object of desire, but, shucks: Fuck off."

Braddock turned and yelled back down the bar. "Cancel that double, honey, and bring me amyl nitrite."

Connie smiled back at him. She hadn't given the drink a thought. Braddock turned back to Windrow.

"Straight ingrate," he said pleasantly enough. His water and lime arrived. He ignored it, though Windrow turned to watch the bubbles in it. They soothed him, somehow, as they made their way up the sides of the glass, around the ice cubes and the green wedge of lime, to the top.

"So what's with you, Marty. Slip in the bathtub?"

"Got bounced off a case that wasn't even mine, hit the sidewalk on the way out."

"Any interesting legal, social, or moral angles, kinks or precedents?"

"Oh, *lots*. Modern divorce, for one. Nobody's sure, but it's easy. Easier than figuring it out, I guess."

"Listen, Marty. You know what's wrong with marriage? It's *boring*, that's what. One of my absolutely favorite lovers is the macho type that's high up in the police department. You know the type . . ."

Windrow knew the type. And the story.

"His marriage was on the rocks until he met me. Now he sees me once a month—or more—and says his marriage has absolutely turned around since he goes both ways."

Braddock was getting himself worked up. He sipped his drink. Windrow had crossed his arms on the bar and put his chin on them.

61

"You know? I mean, the straightest people are discovering that to be true. They find something lacking in their lives, something missing. They try a little booze, maybe a little pot, a little adultery. Nothing. Then, one night they're a little high, they meet somebody they like, the moon is full . . . 'But that's *queer*,' the good little voice inside them says, 'that's *homosexual*.' 'Oh, what the hell,' the bad voice says. 'Let's get *down*. A little weird sex, dirty sex, filthy sex, maybe some S and M . . . it can't hurt.' "

Braddock took a sip of his water and shrugged. "So they do it. And you know what? They like it. It turns their heads around about things, like sex, and then about certain oppressed groups, and then politics. . . . And you know, they're just the straightest people. I mean, they go to work every day, keep a tidy home, don't drink or smoke, they're registered to vote—"

"Aha," said Windrow.

"Take this one case I know. He's an accountant. Just an accountant. Been with the same firm for ten years, got a wife, two kids. One day he just flips out, For ten years it's been the same old thing with the missus. He's been cutting out with the girls at the office, sure, but, you know, they're built the same as momma. So what's he do?"

Windrow straightened up. "He calls you, Hanfield," he said wearily. "You're in the Yellow Pages, right?"

Braddock giggled. "Well," he said coyly. "I may as well be. So sure. He tries other men, he tries the boys, groups, a little flagellation . . . back to the girls. Presto! he finds out he's into tying up with the girls . . ."

Windrow yawned. "So is his old lady into this?"

"Well, yeah, she's loose, they're modern, she gives it a try. Only she doesn't like it as much as he does, so he still gets around, and that's okay, cause"—Braddock winked—"he's quite a hunk, really. And every now and again he has a, uh, how you say . . ."

"Regression?"

Braddock patted Windrow on the shoulder and let his hand linger there, gently massaging Windrow's shoulder muscle. "That's just the word, Martin. My, but you're astute."

"But how can I be so straight?"

"Right again."

"I hear bells."

"Ever heard Big Ben?"

"That's enough, Hanfield."

Braddock removed his hand. "It's just a shame . . ." His voice trailed off.

Windrow patted Braddock on the shoulder. "It's okay, Hand. When they get the clone thing together, I'll get one of me made up just for you." Windrow took a sip of whiskey. "Right after I get the one that does my job for me."

"That'll be nice," Braddock said dreamily. "But I was talking about the girl."

Windrow raised his beer glass to his lips. "What girl?"

"Oh, just a girl I knew. A real tragedy. This guy I was telling you about ran around with her for a while. He got her into the scene a little bit, too, I guess. I mean the straight tie-up thing. They were a nice couple, I thought, but they had to be careful. Low profile. They worked in the same office together, someplace where fraternizing"—Braddock giggled—"among the employees wasn't permitted. Much less tying each other up."

A funny feeling overtook Windrow as he set his untasted glass of beer down on the counter in front of him, a feeling as if his nausea might return, a tingling in his sternum.

"What's so tragic about that?"

Braddock waved his hand and picked up his drink. "Oh, I don't know," he said. "It's just that you can't help thinking that if certain relatively harmless things were more openly permitted, certain relatively horrible things might not happen. It's hard to tell, though."

"What horrible things?"

"Oh, I'm sorry I brought the whole thing up. This girl, after she and this young man broke up, I guess she had gotten a taste for the scene and got mixed up with the wrong sort of people, looking for a bit more of it. I don't know. They found her dead. She'd been horribly brutalized and committed suicide on account of it. That's how it looked, anyway. What a mess."

Windrow watched Braddock in the mirror behind the bottles. "What was her name?" he said.

"Virginia," said Braddock.

"Sarapath," said Windrow.

"Could be," said Braddock. "You should know." Pouring a piece of ice out of his glass into his mouth, he caught Windrow's eye in the mirror. Windrow exhaled long and hard and sat silently looking at his drink for a long time. Braddock chewed up all the ice in his glass and ordered another for himself and Windrow, then sat patiently, watching the two women play pool in the mirror.

Finally, Windrow spoke into his drink.

"What's this guy's name?"

"Sam Driscoll."

Windrow pulled the little notebook out of his pocket and consulted it. "He work for P. J. Brodine, Incorporated?"

Braddock nodded. "The police have already talked to him. They got nothing. After a while, he admitted they'd had an affair, they got that much from her sister. But said they hadn't seen each other in months, outside of work. He was shocked at what had happened, and took the day off from work. That was yesterday. He was in the Diogenes last night."

Windrow put the notebook down on the bar.

"I've been ordered off the case."

"Bdeniowitz hates your guts."

"Do tell."

"But if you have a client . . ."

"What client. I was trying to do a girl a favor."

"What girl?"

"The sister, Marilyn. She's a good kid, been up and down, liked her sister. I like her. But I can't push against Bdeniowitz."

Braddock reached into his pocket and pulled out a hundred-dollar bill and laid it on the counter in front of Windrow.

"I represent interests who would like to see this case cleared up, no matter what," he said.

"What interests?"

"Well, a sort of informal committee, a community group." He waved his hand. "The lady who owns this bar is one of them. I'm another. We put up the money, you work for us. I can get you a list of us, if you want."

Windrow looked at the hundred. "Your word's good enough."

"By the way," said Braddock, "my connections at police headquarters are in much better shape than yours. Anything you need to know, just give me time for a few calls. You can reach me here." He neatly printed his initials and a phone number on Windrow's pad. He grinned. "Day or night."

"Night is when it doesn't hurt so much, right?"

"Which?"

"Never mind."

"He goes to Diogenes every night, after nine."

Braddock gave Windrow a brief description of Driscoll.

"Why the hundred, Hand? What's in it for you?"

"Bdeniowitz is okay, Marty, but some of his cohorts on the force and around city hall, the people who tell him what to do, they don't like the gay world—they hate us, the queens. The cops could use this case to walk all over our community. They may be narrow-minded, but they're not stupid. They couldn't care less, one way or the other, who sleeps with who in this town. But gay people are getting into a lot of political clout in San Francisco, enough so that a lot of straight politicos feel threatened. One way of discrediting an opponent is just as good as another way, to some people. If this case were to erupt into a scandal, good people in our community could be badly hurt for the wrong reasons. A career could be ruined not because of the issues, but because of sexual predilections, or worse, by association.

"When a gay gets castrated in a back alley in this town, the papers don't even mention it, even when there've been four other cases just like it in a month. But when this nice, straight single girl gets it, she makes page one, and there's some sexual weirdo out there, ready to do it again. Now, I'm not questioning that the person's got to be found, but

65

the cops like to act like they think all the butchers are hiding out in the gay scene, and they wouldn't hesitate to run in all two hundred thousand of the homosexuals in this town if they thought they could get away with it.

"What we want from you is hard information that might lead to the truth of who did what to whom and why. Another thing, I want an exclusive for the *Bat*. The paper kicked in for your fees, too. But what I really want is the guy that killed that girl. I met her, you know. She was nice, innocent. If she was into kinky sex I'm sure it was mild, just for fun. I know, I know, I make a lot of noise about the hard stuff, and that's my business. But this girl was nice—plain and simple as that. Some creep got ahold of her and violated that, and much more. The guy's sick. He could probably be helped. He might even want help. See if you can find him before he does it to somebody else."

"Deal." Windrow sipped his drink. "Ever run into anybody carries a sword cane?"

"Oh, dozens," Braddock said. "Very chic."

"This particular party runs a little magazine, your digest of thrills induced by horror and the macabre, *Brandish*."

"Harry Feyn," Braddock nodded. "Used to pen one of those stories occasionally myself. Two cents a word, and not just any word, Harry likes to say, or think. Not so much money in it as real estate, at least not for the writer. Feyn makes out very nicely."

"How about Herbert Trimble?"

"The writer? Plays the cello? Sure. He and Feyn are friends."

"And his wife?"

"Wife, too. They're all friends. Confidentially, sweetie, they had a thing going, you know, a *ménage*, the works. Extra couples, movies." Braddock waved his hand. "You should see Harry's basement. I hear Herbert gave it up, though. Too stiff on Monday morning, he said, but I think it had more to do with his wife's leaving. She quit the whole scene."

"When, this morning?"

"Oh, no, Marty. Honey Trimble dropped out of sight over a year ago. At least that's the last time I saw her."

Windrow was getting that feeling again, compounded by that other one, the nasty one.

"A year ago?" he repeated weakly.

"Yes, about then. In fact they used to drive up from Palo Alto to hang out together at Diogenes. That was the last place I saw her."

"What does she look like?"

"Oh, you name it. But generally I'd say medium height, in her forties, brunette, large in the bosom, tinny voice, triangular glasses . . ."

"Oh, boy," said Windrow faintly.

"Why? You seen her lately?"

"She filed for divorce."

"Really."

"But when I met her, it was last night, and she was flashy. She was tall, with a square face, not big at all in the chest, peroxide hair . . ."

Braddock's puzzled expression hovered a moment between perplexity and a question then gradually resolved itself into a big grin.

"Oh!" Braddock laughed and slapped the bar with his hand. "That wasn't Honey, that was Herbert. That used to be his favorite drag, silly boy!"

Windrow, trying to appear naive, turned to look at Braddock. "His what?"

"His drag! He used to dress up as a peroxide blonde and go dancing in the straightest country-western bars in town. Some drunk would pick him up every time, Herbert was so foxy. Herbert would go with the guy, turn the trick, and a half-hour later the cowboy would be back in the bar swearing it was the best he'd ever had." Braddock cackled and took a quick sip of bubble water. "Brilliant man," he added, "He has these delicious foibles."

Windrow looked at himself in the mirror. Braddock's laughter tapered off, and he looked at Windrow thoughtfully. Gradually, his amusement returned, reinforced.

"You?" he said and pointed at Windrow. "You and some big blonde—"

"It's not like you think, Hanfield."

"Hah! Oh that's rich, rich, just too, *too* much. . . ." Braddock dissolved into laughter, He came up for air long enough to say, "And we hired you, a *detective*. Oh, hoo hoo hoo . . ."

"I'll take care of the case," Windrow said, coloring.

"Some private dick you turned out to be, ahh . . ." Braddock was coughing and laughing. Windrow silently hoped he'd choke.

"There's—there's just one thing, Marty," Braddock said through his tears, trying to catch his breath. He put his hand on Windrow's shoulder and leaned closer.

"Yeah?" said Windrow, rigid. "What's that, Hanfield?"

"Why not me, baby? Why'd you throw it away on that big, ugly queen?"

"It ain't like you think, Hanfield."

"Aw, that's okay, Marty, I can take it. But now that you're out, you big handsome hunk you, don't you think you could spare a little for your old sweetheart Hanny? Hmmm?"

"Knock it off, Braddock. I just had breakfast."

"Aw . . . Come on, Marty-poo, just one little trick, out back, in the alley . . . ?"

Chapter Twelve

When Windrow came out of the package store on Folsom Street with a large pair of grocery bags in his arms, he had to wedge his way through the three ladies crowding the doorway.

"Don't you girls ever work?" he said gaining the sidewalk.

One of the two black hookers eyed him sullenly. "I smell money," she said.

"It's catnip," Windrow said over his shoulder.

"Meow," the white hooker said.

Windrow jaywalked backward halfway across Folsom Street, watching the girls. One of them rubbed her belly and licked her lips. Windrow turned 540°, let a truck go by, and made the curb in front of his so-called office building. When respectable clients came downtown to hire him, they usually never even got out of the cab. They went right out to the Avenues and paid the higher fees.

But the girls made him feel good. They knew he had four twenties in his pocket and some change. They were rarely wrong about such things. Just the thought of it, the remote possibility that the money might easily become theirs, cheered them. Once after a particularly big case Windrow had danced out of the liquor store with his arms full of shopping bags and given them a twenty apiece, asking nothing in return. They were astonished. Just the day before they'd seen him buy a loaf of sourdough bread, two eggs, and two cans of beer on credit. Next thing they know he's leafletting them with twenties and telling them to take the day off. They hadn't, of course. Each had tucked away her bill folded twice, and stayed on the job.

Upstairs Windrow emptied one bag into his refrigerator, leaving out an unmarked plastic bag full of fresh taco chips, a quart yogurt tub full of fresh guacamole, a dozen eggs, a lemon, and a newspaper. Out of the other bag came beer, a pint of whiskey, and a bottle of aspirin. Humming to himself, he dressed a can of Tecate by rubbing a slice of lemon all over the top of the can and pouring salt on top of that. Licking the rim, he took a long swallow. He dipped a large taco chip into the guacamole and, humming and chewing, sat himself down behind his desk in the swivel chair. He dialed a number.

"Emmy? Marty. Papers delivered. Bill's in the mail. What? My office. Listen. What did Mrs. Trimble look like? Blonde? Big? Sexy clothes? No chest? Yeah. Okay. That wasn't Mrs. Trimble. I said that wasn't Mrs. Trimble. What? Well, I think it was Mr. Trimble. Right, he wants a divorce from himself. Well, give him credit for trying. No, I don't know why. Nobody's seen her. Medium height, a hundred thirty pounds, brunette, favors triangular glasses. Into the kinky sex. Yeah, a pair. Well, three of them, actually, counting the second Mrs. Trimble. Harry Feyn makes it a foursome. Editor of a magazine called *Brandish*. What? You *know* him? Sure, I'll hang on."

Windrow stood up and leaned over the desk to get another chip full of guacamole. His mouth was still full when he said, "Yeah, I'm still here." He listened for a long time. Emmy Cohen was telling him that Harry Feyn had twice been a client of hers. In each case, someone had filed charges against Feyn for assault, and in each case, the charges had been dropped.

The first person had been Mrs. Trimble.

The second person had been Sammy Driscoll.

Windrow's rapid chewing slowed to a cow's pace, then stopped altogether. "Wait, Emmy, wait. What were the circumstances?" He heard the rustle of files at the other end of the phone. Driscoll had dropped the charges; Mrs. Trimble had failed to show up in court.

"So you never saw Mrs. Trimble for the first time? Right. But when she came to you about the divorce she said Feyne had recommended you? Did she say anything else? Nothing. Man, I don't know what it means. Sure. I'll let you know." He hung up.

Windrow swiveled his chair so that he faced the window on to the street.

So the loose ends were suddenly tying knots with each other, all by themselves. From a zero, first thing in the morning, he'd piled up a new client and more leads than he could follow in one day.

Harry Feyn knows the Trimbles, and Harry Feyn knows Sam Driscoll. There is at the moment no connection between Driscoll and the Trimbles, except that Driscoll brought charges aainst Feyn and would have had to deal with Emmy Cohen through Feyn. Virginia Sarapath knew Driscoll and lived next door to Trimble. Virginia Sarapath had no connection to Feyn, except that she knew Driscoll fairly well and lived next door to Feyn's other buddy, Trimble. No matter which way you turned when you left Virginia Sarapath's house, the paths led to Feyn.

Virginia was new in town. Even though she was pretty, she didn't have any real friends. She didn't get along well enough with her sister to do things with her socially; she didn't like to drink. Windrow hadn't noticed any booze in her apartment, whereas in Marilyn's place there was plenty of evidence of it. Like in her eyes.

So she meets this guy Driscoll. Driscoll looks like a nice man, but he's on the lam from his wife. All he really wants to do is score. More than that, he wants to score in unusual ways. Virginia's not too sure at first and no doubt he's cagey about it—at first. Then he makes his play. Will she let him tie her up? Naked? Maybe whip her or knock her around a bit?

If she says no, he backs down right away, tries later, or maybe even turns it around. He makes a joke out of it. Well, look. Why doesn't she tie *him* up? Look, just tighten this knot a bit. See? It's fun . . .

Maybe she's turned off, or scared. If not sooner, then later. Besides, not only is this guy kinky, he's married. No matter what happens, she gets hurt, in more ways than one. So she gets out. Relations are strained at the office, but eventually things calm down. Then, whammo! Someone beats her up so badly she cuts her wrists with a razor. If it had been a prowler, even a rapist, it might not have happened. She would have gone for help.

A thought struck Windrow. What if it did happen like that? What if the sadist was a man completely unknown to her and she went to Trimble for help? And Trimble, seeing her condition, refused to have anything to do with her—or did it to her all over again? Then she would have killed herself. Out of despair.

But Trimble didn't look either type. He was crazy as a loon, no doubt about it. But something about his story, or what Windrow had heard of it, rang true. Trimble probably did try to mind his own business, for as long as possible, until the scene next door had become too much to bear. Trimble was a sensitive man. He was a normal citizen in certain respects, too. A city boy, he'd seen plenty. If the girl next door liked to get beaten up in her spare time, that would be okay with him. But something, some noice or something in her voice, had made him go next door.

71

What had Herbert Trimble found there?

Windrow opened another Tecate, dressed it and returned to his chair with a chipful of guacamole.

It seemed more likely, given her slight experience in the scene, that Virginia knew whoever it was who had beaten her so severely. That she had then either killed herself out of humiliation, or . . .

Or it had been faked.

Windrow put the nails in the horseshoe she saw in his mind's eye. Sarapath, Driscoll, Feyn, Trimble. Trimble, Feyn, Driscoll, Sarapath.

This guy Feyn knows everybody in town. Did he know Virginia Sarapath? He certainly reacted strongly to her name. Had that been his conception of his part of playing Herbert Trimble? Why had he been in the house with Trimble when Windrow had visited there? Why had he hidden himself? Was he just waiting for Herbert to score a trick? Or did he have more than that to hide? Was the trick a ruse? Why should he even bother to be involved with the Sarapath case? Why didn't he just throw Herbert Trimble to the wolves—or at least let him be interrogated? After all, if Herbert were innocent . . .

Or was he so innocent? Windrow suddenly remembered the bruises on Mrs. Trimble's throat, ineffectually hidden by the gaudy collar with the rectangular links. Herbert had worn a cravat this morning; obviously, since he and "Mrs. Trimble" were the same person, his neck would sport the same bruises. From what he had heard, Trimble must like to get bruised up, once in a while. Or had someone tried to strangle Trimble?

Another thing. Virginia Sarapath's neck had bruises on it. Had Virginia and Herbert fallen into the hands of the same person? Or just the same *technique*?

And where, where is the real Mrs. Trimble? She must be a very interesting person.

Windrow picked up the phone and dialed the number given him by Hanfield Braddock.

"Hanny? Windrow. No, I haven't changed my mind. Listen. I need to talk to someone in the morgue who knows what's going on down there. My office. Okay." He hung up.

Five minutes later the phone rang.

"Mr. Windrow?"

"Speaking."

"This is Michael, down at the county morgue. I understand you have a question?"

"Yes, Michael. You got any unidentified stiffs down there?"

"Always."

"Female."

"Um, four."

"Caucasian."

"Two."

"Brunette, about a hundred thirty pounds . . ."

"That leaves one."

"Would a photo do it?"

"Nope. Came out of the bay. She's almost completely decomposed."

"Could you match a dental chart?"

"Sure, give me a place to start."

"I'll get back to you."

Windrow hung up and dialed Braddock's number gain.

"Hello?"

"Dentists."

"Charming people. They always have nitrous oxide, cocaine, those little tools . . ."

"Palo Alto dentists. Menlo Park, Portola Valley. In a hurry, it's late."

"You just had breakfast."

"It's two o'clock. I gotta know."

"I'll get back to you." Braddock hung up.

This one took a little longer. Windrow opened another Tecate and finished the guacamole, sitting in front of his window. After half an hour, the phone rang. The caller identified himself as Dennis the dentist. Windrow told him what he needed. The fellow was most obliging. Dennis the dentist would see what he could do. He hung up, and Windrow, taking a Tecate with him, curled up on his sofa for a nap.

73

The telephone woke him up at a quarter to six. It was Michael, morgue Michael.

"Mr. Windrow? The charts arrived a little while ago. The city didn't have an account with the messenger service . . ."

"What? Did you pay him?"

"Yes, sir. Since you're a friend of Walter's . . ."

"Walter? Walter—Oh. Oh, yeah, Walter. Well, Michael, you did good. Just send me a bill. Six-eight-two Folsom Street."

"Oh, that's not necessary, Mr. Windrow. I could just bring it over, after work. I'm just up the street. We could have a drink . . ."

"That's okay, Michael, just send me the bill, like I said. I'm, uh, all pledged up tonight."

Michael was quiet for a moment.

"You get that address?"

"Uh, sure, Mr. Windrow." Michael sounded hurt.

"What about the dental plates?"

"You must be onto something, Mr. Windrow. It's a match. Both the uppers and lowers, except for one filling that could have been done later. And two broken teeth."

"Broken teeth? Where?"

"Left front. Canine and incisor."

"Like from a severe blow, maybe?"

"I'm not the pathologist, Mr. Windrow, but yes, they may have been broken like that."

"Cause of death?"

"Hard to tell. Might have been internal injuries or poison or something like that. Nothing to show for it outside the two teeth, but they haven't run extensive tests yet either. They just brought her in last week . . ."

"How long has she been in the drink?"

"Maybe two to six months."

"Can't you get any more precise than that Michael?"

"We'd have to be authorized to make more tests, Mr. Windrow."

"Okay, Michael. You've done very well. I appreciate your help and talent. Now I want you to do one more thing for me. Take those matching charts, the name of the dentist, and whatever else you have upstairs and give them to Captain Bdeniowitz in homicide."

"Yes, Mr. Windrow. Is he a friend of yours?"

"Never mind that. Just take them up there, kid. And thanks."

"Whatever you say, Mr. Windrow. Please give my best to Walter."

"Walt—? Oh. Oh yeah. I will. Oh and Michael."

The kid was all ears. "Yes, Mr. Windrow?"

"Give that bill to Bdeniowitz. If he won't pay it send it to me." Windrow hung up.

He had found Honey Trimble.

Chapter Thirteen

The disappearance of Honey Trimble, her probable murder, made things look bleak indeed for Herbert Trimble. Herbert would be looked upon as having been entirely too close, physically proximate, to two grisly events, to be anything but guiltless; Bdeniowitz would never turn loose until he had built up some kind of a case against Trimble, for murder one plus one. Windrow himself thought that at the very least Trimble constituted the best if not the single, material witness in the Sarapath case; and it seemed to him well-nigh impossible that Trimble should know nothing about his wife's demise.

The more Windrow looked into the Trimbles' backgrounds, the more it looked as if Mrs. Trimble's disappearance had coincided with their move to San Francisco. After just a few phone calls, beginning with one to Trimble's Palo Alto dentist, then one each to the museum director's secretary, the director himself, a co-worker, and a bartender who had regularly served Mrs. Trimble her Brandy Alexanders, a pattern showed its edges. The Trimbles had known a few people around Palo Alto and Menlo Park, had even had one or two close friends, chiefly among the museum staff, and had seen them on a more or less routine basis right up until the time they left town. After the move, nothing. No one among the people Windrow could find could remember seeing Mrs. Trimble after the Trimbles went to the city for good. Herbert had shown up occasionally, to use the museum library. And he had commuted to Menlo Park two nights a week for a month to complete rehearsals with a small community orchestra and, finally, to perform with them for two nights. The piece was Edward Elgar's cello concerto, and Herbert was the solo cellist. To his ex-co-worker from the museum, who had attended the performance, Herbert had movingly described the performance as the high point of his life.

Honey hadn't been able to make the date.

It was during these telephone calls, in the course of mulling these odd bits of information that Martin Windrow firmed up his opinion of Herbert Trimble. First he decided, anybody who could play the solo instrument in Edward Elgar's cello concerto, or any other instrument in the orchestra, for that matter, couldn't be all bad. His associates described him as a brilliant, gentle man, whose moods—eccentric, ephemeral—they tolerated or overlooked entirely.

Second, he began to believe that Herbert Trimble's life was in danger.

With the whistling cry of the red-tailed hawk, Windrow's mind circled up out of his office and over the city. In his mind's hawk's eye he saw the slopes of the city, its neighborhoods, a certain street, a particular building, the specific apartment.

He needed answers. The ends and pieces of this case were raveling busily, but he couldn't yet pick out their meaning or direction.

The cops had already checked Driscoll out and gotten nowhere. A phone call to Gleason at home got the story.

They'd found Mrs. Driscoll, seen the three kids, in Walnut Creek, across the Bay Bridge. She'd answered their questions with a few impatient monosyllables, all negative, and sent them back across the bridge with the address of a studio apartment on Franklin Street near Washington. They'd caught him at home, to be polite, they said. They told him they knew of his connection to Ms. Sarapath, and would rather not have to embarrass him at the office with a lot of questions about their relationship. Would he mind cooperating? Of course not. Most appreciative. Well, Driscoll said, he and Virginia had a little eyeball contact over the account books, and a little physical contact in the elevator. Then came a walk to the bus stop. A few nights later the walk stopped into a bar for a drink; a few nights after that it was two drinks. Then drinks and dinner. Then the next night drinks, dinner, more drinks, a short cab ride to Driscoll's apartment and well, gentlemen, we are men of the world, a spread of the hands, et cetera.

Driscoll claimed they had slept together twice, maybe three times; it hadn't meant much to him, and he couldn't remember when exactly. She'd never stayed the entire night with him, but only because he wouldn't let her. She had gotten too serious very fast and he'd had to explain to her he wasn't ready for that kind of responsibility; he'd just been through a marriage. He just wanted a few laughs, a little sex, some sneaking around the office. She took it hard. She was a lonely girl in the big city and wanted someone firmly established in her life. Breaking off proved to be messy. They'd even convened a bitter, tearful argument in hoarse whispers in a stairwell at work. It'd been difficult for her, Driscoll had said, but eventually Virginia had gotten over him and they remained civil to each other in the office. He had patiently explained to the two deadpan detectives, Gleason and Bdeniowitz, that it was the old story of a young, inexperienced woman becoming overly enamored of an older, experienced man. Her expectations and hopes for the relationship had far exceeded his own, he told them. After he'd let her down as easily as possible and helped her through the emotional pain, they'd stopped meeting. They hadn't seen each other outside the office for several months. When she didn't show up for work on Monday and didn't call, he'd tried to call her that night. No answer. That was that, until he read the Tuesday *Chronicle*.

Gleason was unimpressed, and drinking beer. "Guy thinks he's a *Playgirl* foldout," he said rather thickly, "but he's a fish." A beer can clicked against the mouthpiece of Gleason's telephone. "Hey, you should see that crummy sheetrock studio of his. It looks worse than mine, for God-sakes. There's plastic everywhere; there's plastic on the ceilings, for Chrissakes. The plastic on the floor he calls fur-niture; the plastic on the walls he calls art; and the plastic out the window he calls his 'view.' And you know what he calls that place? His 'pee-ed ah tair,' man. 'Pee-ed ah tair,' my ass, Marty."

Windrow heard the crash of a beer can as it hit the refrig-erator and ricocheted into the metal trash can beneath it, across the room from the table on which Gleason kept his telephone. In the background he could hear the Giants get-ting whipped on national television. "Pee-ed ah tair. It might have been funny except this guy takes himself seri-ously. The guy's got his feet on his neck, man. Shoes between his ears. He's clean, though. Clean as any playboy of the Western world. We asked around. The manager had seen the Sarapath girl there once; the old lady in the down-stairs front had seen her twice. Nobody had seen her lately. Trimble's number one on our tote, Marty. All we gotta do is find him. When we do, we'll sweat it out of him."

Windrow obtained the address of Driscoll's love nest and a description, then rang off.

So Gleason hadn't yet heard about Honey Trimble. Bde-niowitz probably wouldn't tell him, then he'd blow a fuse when Gleason didn't know a thing about it. He might even bless him out in front of the rest of the department for being stupid and neglecting his duty.

And Harry Feyn had entered the police picture by mis-take, and they'd apologized to him for it. The death of Honey Trimble would only make it the worse for Herbert, and if Herbert was innocent, as Windrow thought, it was possible he was being set up as the kinky, unbalanced, homicidal, amnesiac fall guy.

It was either that, Windrow thought, looking out the win-dow at the whores—two of them now, under the lights of the liquor store across the street—or Trimble was a hell of an actor. That was possible, too. The guy had the talent for it and the stakes were plenty high. Whoever Trimble was playing to—himself, Windrow, Feyn, the cops—he was playing for his life.

So far, outside simple geography, there was still only one connection between Trimble and Driscoll. Harry Feyn, the man with the sword cane. Harry Feyn probably had all the answers, or most of them. But he obviously preferred not to hand out information for free. If Windrow wanted to get anything out of Feyn—and it looked to Windrow like Feyn was the man with the handles—Windrow would need leverage. Leverage meant evidence. Hard evidence, something even the police were short of. Their case consisted entirely of figures drawn by hands waving in thin air, as if by sparklers whirling in a dark night, just as much as Windrow's did. But Windrow had noticed the magazines in Trimble's apartment. He had accidentally talked to Feyn, on the street in front of Honey Trimble's house. He had met Trimble in both his drags. On a hunch he had discovered that Mrs. Trimble was dead, very likely murdered. He had a witness who had seen Sammy Driscoll in the company of Virginia Sarapath recently, perhaps more recently than Driscoll had been willing to admit to the cops. They'd been seen in a joint that was known to cater to people in the leather scene, an angle that no cop was aware of, outside of the fact that the Sarapath girl's body showed the signs of deliberate sadism. What did it all add up to?

Feeling in his coat pockets, Windrow found the old black-and-white photograph of Harry Feyn that the she-Trimble had given him. He studied it. The man in it looked bored, restless, and possibly distracted, just as he'd looked when Windrow first saw the picture. He hadn't expected it to change. Perhaps, it was just possible that, he'd misread the expression on the man's face as distracted. It could be the look of a man building fantasies on the floor at the photographer's feet. Harry Feyn might be a dreamer or a megalomaniac or drunk.

Dropping the picture on the desk behind him, Windrow put both his hands behind his head, and clasped the back of his head with them. Inadvertently, the heel of his left hand rubbed smartly against the knot on the back of his head. He said "Ow," softly and winced and swore. That was when he remembered it. He dropped his feet off the windowsill, sat up in the chair, and spun around as his feet hit the floor. The sudden gesture disturbed his broken rib, tugged at all of this stitches, and made his eyes smart in their sockets. But he retrieved the photograph, peered at it under the desk lamp, and there it was.

The picture album.

He remembered seeing it the first time he'd looked at the photograph, when Trimble had handed it to him at Honey's house. Now he noticed again that the partially exposed album, lying on a table covered with bottles and glasses behind the couch in the picture, looked the same as the album from which he'd watched Trimble extract the picture he now held in his hand. The table was gone, the furniture had been rearranged, time had passed, but the Trimbles still had their photo album. It was a fat white, vinyl-bound book, full of memories from their years together. It would start with their wedding pictures; it would contain pictures of both their families, of their friends, pictures taken at concerts, events, parties . . . Pictures taken of themselves by other people . . . as they tied each other up . . . He'd seen one of them.

Herbert Trimble, disguised as a woman, calling himself his wife's name, had tried to hand Martin Windrow a photograph of Harry Feyn shackled to a wall.

Windrow had rejected it as it was too weird, he didn't need a picture like that for the purposes of a simple identification. A shot like that in any other part of the world would have been sufficient heft for blackmail, let alone identification. But this was San Francisco; a picture like that in San Francisco was a mild curiosity and little else. In San Francisco, you couldn't blackmail a judge with a picture like that.

So he'd given it back. He hadn't needed it.

But he'd been wrong. Harry Feyn had been somewhere in the house while Windrow was interviewing the person he'd thought was Honey Trimble. When Windrow asked Mrs. Trimble for a picture of her husband, a picture they both knew might put the finger on a murder suspect, Herbert Trimble had handed over a photograph of Harry Feyn, tied up. Harry Feyn, tied up.

It had been a silent plea. A cry for help.

Windrow banged his open palm on the desk and stood up. Of course! Feyn was *there*, probably in the very next room. He could have had a gun trained on both of them, or at the very least he'd had his cane, that sword cane. Trimble couldn't have said a word without endangering himself or Windrow or both of them, because Windrow hadn't a clue to what was going on. He'd caught them at that house; for some reason they had needed to be there, and Trimble was supposed to get rid of Windrow or distract him. Hence the big sex act.

But Trimble wasn't dumb. Windrow was the dumb one. Windrow was so goddamn dumb he ought to quit now and beg the City to let him spend the rest of his life quietly raking leaves, deep in Golden Gate Park. Trimble had figured out a way to tell the whole story, and Windrow hadn't noticed it. For *two days* he hadn't noticed it and it had been in his coat pocket the whole time.

Windrow paced feverishly back to his desk and picked up the picture. The album. There it is. If there were enough pictures in that scrapbook to include one of Feyn naked, chained to a wall, and one of him fully dressed at a party, acting more or less normal, then there must be more, many more interesting pictures in the white album. It would only take one snapshot along the lines of that first one of Feyn to form the last and final link in the deadly chain that stretched from Virginia Sarapath through Samuel Driscoll, Harry Feyn, and Honey Trimble to Herbert Trimble, and back again to Virginia Sarapath. If it existed, such a picture would be circumstantial, but it would be another piece in the story, and maybe, just maybe, it would constitute evidence.

81

Chapter Fourteen

He parked the Toyota a block away from Honey Trimble's house, at the top of the hill where Seventeenth Street crossed Clayton, and sat in it, watching the neighborhood.

Beyond the top of Claytlon Street where it began its descent toward upper Market Street and much higher, stood the immense tripod of the Sutro Tower. Normally, day or night you could see the tower from almost anywhere in town. At night its red warning lights blinked irregularly up and down its legs, from the footings to the very tips of the antennae at its top, but this night the fog had rolled in from the Pacific; it had crested the hill on which Sutro Tower stood and tumbled down into the valley, all the way down to Market Street, south and east of Market, past Windrow's tiny office, past the Ferry Building, past the docks and piers, back to the interior waters of the bay. Here the fog, having also penetrated inland by following the meandering shoreline and sea-level surfaces of the bay waters through the Golden Gate, joined itself again. Like the foghorns—the "moaners" atop navigation buoys, the timed, lugubrious horns used by anchored shipping vessels—Sutro Tower and the very far end of the city block on which Windrow had parked were completely invisible, swallowed into the billowing, thick, salt-tanged mists that had enveloped most of the city.

It looked like a perfect night for burglary. The night would give him cover, and the fog would help in that, too; not only would visibility be difficult, but the fog affected sound in strange ways. A noise made a block away might sound as if it were just next door, and a piece of glass dropped on a roof might never be heard at all. Windrow would be needing that sort of help; he welcomed it and wished he had more. He could, for example, employ a nice little diversion, for he knew the police would be watching the house he intended to burglarize. Trimble's house hadn't been staked out the last time Windrow had visited it, but now, with a double murder hanging over the person the police had actually interviewed there after the discovery of the first murder, they would not allow themselves a chance for a slip-up again. The house would be watched.

Switching over to the passenger seat, Windrow removed his shoes, his coat and his shoulder harness. Over his feet he tied a pair of black running shoes. In place of his coat he wore an old hunting vest which had large game pockets, inside and out, and the smaller chest pockets with loops sewn over them for shotgun shells, and over that an old overcoat that had two pockets on the outside and two inside. Into these pockets, he placed a variety of tools, selected from a tackle box on the floorboard between his feet, and a larger toolbox on the backseat. These included a small roll of gray duct tape; a hank of nylon rope; his incomplete collection of passkeys; a glass cutter; a small ball of nylon mason's twine; a Swiss army knife; three tapered wooden wedges; a flat prybar about twelve inches long, two pieces of stiff plastic, about the same dimensions as common charge cards, except for their longer length; a ruler, made of thin flexible steel, one foot long; a penlight, which he tested before stowing it away in his bulging pockets; and a pair of thin, cotton work gloves, dark brown.

He placed the tools around his pockets so that they wouldn't make too much noise when he moved and so that their weight hung from him in as balanced a fashion as possible. After he had distributed them, he fingered each tool in its pocket, remembering where each piece of equipment was located. While humming "The Battle of New Orleans," he removed the Toyota key from its ring and put the ring and remaining keys along with all his change and wallet into the glove compartment. Getting out of the car, he took off his watch and checked it—11:30—and laid it on the seat. He locked the passenger door, dropped the single key into his watch pocket, and walked to the intersection of Seventeenth and Clayton Streets.

There was very little traffic, and he jaywalked across

Seventeenth and continued along Clayton Street. The fog-horns floated up to him from the bay, and he could almost hear the fog's thick moisture as it impinged on his coat and on the leaves of the tree lined street. When he reached the top of the hill he crossed Clayton Street and walked down the hill on the side of the street opposite the Trimble home. Hands jammed in the deep, tool-filled pockets of his coat, his collar up as if against the cool, penetrating breath of the fog, he walked purposefully, a man with someplace to go.

A third of the way down the block, as he'd begun to round the outside of the curve that didn't straighten out until it had crossed Corbett Street at the bottom of the block, the Trimble home came into sight. A tall pine in front of it partially obscured his view, but Windrow could see that though the front porch was lit, no light showed from inside the house. He slowed his pace, but not too much, and studied the street in front of the house. There were cars up and down the block, on both sides of the street. He couldn't see an empty parking place. Most of the front and rear windows of these vehicles had fog on them. This was bad. He had to know where the stake out was before he tried to enter the Trimble house. All the luck and little skill he had in breaking and entering might be sufficient to get him inside the house, find the photo album, and get safely out and away with it, but to attempt to enter the house without knowing where the stakeout was would be foolish. He could discern no signs of life in any of the cars on the other side of the street. As he walked past the ones on his side of the street he looked into each as closely as he dared, without being too obvious.

He drew even with the Trimble house. Still he'd seen nothing. With each step the house floated further back up the hill, behind him, and still he saw nothing. As he'd walked down the street he'd identified the cars parked there. There'd been a few Porsches, a Triumph, a Cadillac, lots of Volkswagens, Pintos, and Japanese cars, and these he felt he could eliminate. The police department favored plain, medium-sized American sedans. There'd been one such car toward the top of the block, but in the dark he hadn't been able to discern anything through the wet windows.

If he couldn't spot the stakeout he may as well go home. In the morning he'd have to figure out a way to get to Bdeniowitz, and then convince the man he had a good hunch. There'd be a search warrant to obtain, then the search. After it was over, Bdeniowitz was perfectly capable of keeping whatever he found to himself, cutting Windrow completely out of it, and that was okay, but Bdeniowitz would see the evidence, if any, only in terms of whatsoever weight it might add to his case against Trimble. Windrow would be back in his office, drinking beer and watching the girls across the street and waiting for another idea. He'd have nothing for Braddock and nothing to tell Marilyn.

Of course, it was nothing to Windrow if the gay community got rousted, though a little bonus from Braddock's committee would be nice. And as for Marilyn, nothing Windrow or anybody else might do would bring her sister back. By the look of things, Virginia Sarapath hadn't deserved what she'd gotten, not by a long shot. But she'd gotten death, and a lot more, which brought Windrow to his point. The man—or woman—who had killed and maimed Virginia Sarapath was still out there. There was a chance that the same person had something to do with the death of Honey Trimble—maybe yes, maybe no. There seemed a better chance that the Sarapath murder was not premeditated. It could have been an accident; it could have been an act of passion. True, there were extenuating circumstances: the razor, the dismemberment, the blood on Trimble's doorknob, but they might have been frills, red herring, alum in the bloodhound's nose. The circumstances seemed clumsily stacked against Trimble, almost as if by chance . . .

In any case, the murderer was still at large. He might kill again.

The Trimble house had already slipped back around the corner, up the hill and out of his sight but Windrow, toward the bottom of the hill, could still see the black, year-old Ford parked a few cars down from the top of the hill, across the street from the house. At the last possible moment, as if he were going to walk down Corbett Street when he got to it, Windrow turned to cross the street again. As he did so, he looked up the hill, directly at the black Ford. He saw two things before his pace made the Ford disappear behind the low branches of the closely planted trees and hedges that lined the lower end of the inside of the curve on the next-to-last block on Clayton Street.

He'd seen that the window on the driver's side of the car was cracked open, about two inches; and just before it had disappeared, a thin plume of smoke had drifted out of that crack and up a bit, above the car, smoke clearly defined by the streetlight at the intersection before it swirled and vanished in the fog.

The guy was good. Windrow wondered how and when the man in the car had gotten that cigarette lit, while, no doubt, watching the man in the overcoat stroll down the block. Probably with the car's cigarette lighter, so there was no flare from a match or other type of light for Windrow to spot.

But Windrow had spotted him, and that was all he needed. It seemed very unlikely that the police department would have more than one man on a given shift to spare on the long shot that a murder suspect would make the same stupid move twice. At any rate, that was another chance that Windrow would have to take.

Having crossed Clayton Street, Windrow turned right onto the sidewalk and walked the few remaining yards to the intersection of Corbett and Clayton. He crossed Corbett, then turned left on it and walked to a tree that stood at the head of the bus stop there, and leaned on it. From this intersection, Corbett proceeded steeply down the hill, below Clayton, for about a half-mile, until it joined up with Seventeenth Street, many blocks downhill from the intersection of Seventeenth and Clayton, near which Windrow had parked his car fifteen minutes before. Excepting a few curves, Corbett could be said to form the hypotenuse of a traingle, the ninety-degree vertex of which formed the intersection of Seventeenth and Clayton Streets. From the vertex at which Windrow stood, Corbett angled acutely away and down from Clayton, like a terraced switchback on the side of a mountain. On the high side across the street, Windrow could just make out the clusters of needles in the top of the Monterey pine in front of the Trimble house, their undersides dimly illuminated by the light on the porch.

From the relative neutral zone of the bus stop, Windrow studied carefully the layout of the hill above him, then began to walk leisurely down the side of Corbett opposite the Clayton side. He strolled slowly, his eyes carefully examining every housefront and driveway. At one point he stopped, then walked on. Then he stopped again.

Across the street from him, what looked like a little driveway ran steeply up the hill, perpendicularly away from the street. He crossed and peered up it. The little driveway extended up the hill sharply, between two tall hedges. He walked up it.

At its top, the narrow concrete strip flattened into a small parking area that might have held three cars, and contained none, but it would take a very unusual car to climb up into it. A very small bungalow of perhaps two rooms faced on to the parking area to his left. On his right a series of little storage sheds, four of them, each a little higher up the grade than the one next to it, leaned up the slope. The uphill side of the parking area was bordered by a low retaining wall, beyond which were three small, steep yards, and beyond those, much higher up, three houses towered above him. The one on the right was the Trimble home.

He recognized it by the apartment building that completely filled the lot next to it further uphill on Clayton Street. The large, lit pine stood between them, on the street side. Along the edge of this building, two levels of long balconies provided outdoor access to all of the apartments on that side of the building.

The yards were all badly fenced, with rickety posts and boards and wire that would surely collapse under the weight of anything heavier than a cat. But one of the balconies ended about ten feet above the roof of the uppermost shed to Windrow's right. He walked toward that corner of the flat turning a complete circle as he did so. The bunga-low was dark. There was no one in sight. He stepped up onto the wall, and levered himself up to the roof of the shed, ignoring the stabs of pain in his rib and abdomen. There he swiftly unbuttoned his coat and vest. A short hop allowed him to grasp the lowest railing of the balcony. He swung himself back and forth three times and hooked his left leg up and onto the cement balcony, between its surface and the low railing. With this foothold he used the metal-rod balusters in the railing to pull himself up and onto the walkway.

Quietly, he walked past a room with a dryer turning in it, an apartment with a television on in it, and a dark apart-ment that emanated soft music.

At the end of the walk a staircase of two flights climbed up to the second-level balcony, which led directly to the street. There was a gate across the entrance, lit, and the light from there flooded the second half of the stairs, from the landing up to the street-level walkway. This entrance was immediately adjacent to the pine tree and the entrance to the Trimble's house.

But Windrow was forty feet to the rear of the building from the entrance, and directly above his head, perhaps five feet from the top edge of the walkway above him, was the bottom of a deck that cantilevered off the back of the Trimble house. Stepping onto the guardrail of the lower walkway, he climbed up the outside edges of the exposed treads of the staircase to the first landing and thence, angling toward the back of the building as he went, to the street-level walkway. Not stopping, using a support post he balanced himself on the top of the upper guardrail and, holding on to the post where it hit the eave of the apart-ment building, leaned out as far as he could.

His left hand came a foot short of the redwood post on the outside corner of the Trimble's deck, and a few inches below it. The drop to the sharp slope below was about thirty feet. But Windrow wasn't looking down. As he leaned toward the deck he looked to the right of the enclosed entrance to the house and the barely swaying trunk of the pine tree, through the steel bars of the gate that led onto the walkway below his feet. Dimly, beyond a parked car and across Clayton Street higher up, he could see the black hood of the Ford.

He looked at his left hand. It was clearly illuminated by the light that spilled back from the entrances to the two buildings, between which he hung. As he hesitated a draft from out of the fog sifted through the pine boughs above him. The old tree creaked and the boughs sighed. A pair of needles dropped onto his neck and made him start. As he did so he noticed mottled shadows passing over his exposed wrist. He forced his right hand to turn loose, and as he fell away from the building he jumped for the post.

The left hand grabbed a thin redwood slat, the next in line beyond the post, and his right got the edge of the deck at the corner. There was nothing for it but to lift his right foot up until its heel caught the edge of the deck that ran from the house, on the same edge as the excellent view of the police car out front. His open coat and vest dangled straight down from his nearly horizontal body, but since the pockets were deep and more or less upright, no tools spilled out of them. He hung there a moment.

His right side was his stronger. If he tried to pull himself up with his left, the rib would dig in, his abdomen and buttocks would open up. Sweating and grunting, he was pulling himself up the corner post when he heard the door open and had to freeze.

The noise of the television suddenly got louder, and down on the lower level of the apartment building, someone in bare feet—he could see the feet and lovely legs to the waist—walked the short distance from the last apartment to the laundry room, humming. The tune was "I Wonder Who's Kissing Her Now." As soon as Windrow heard the door of the dryer open and the machine stop, he hauled himself up so that he was crouching on the outside of the deck railing. Seeing no one on the other side, he fell over the rail, using as low a profile as possible, and leaned against the corner post breathing heavily.

His hands were full of redwood splinters, and in spite of

his caution, his abdomen ached. As his breathing slowed, he once again could hear the breeze in the pine tree out front, the foghorns, the television. He peered through the slats of the side railing. The Ford was still there. He could see the windshied and the driver's door. He could even see that the resident of the Ford had wiped the condensation off the window in the door. It was still rolled down about two inches, and the vent window was tilted open.

Below him, Windrow heard the door of the laundry room pulled closed. The legs and bare feet padded back up the walkway, a pillowcase full of laundry dangling beside them. They turned into the first open door, the door closed quietly, the mutter of the television became almost indiscernable.

Windrow looked back at the Ford and waited. His shirt and pants had soaked up most of his perspiration, and now the breeze was cooling him off. He carefully pulled the overcoat closed, and peered again through the slats of the deck, past the corner of the house, over the top of the car parked out front, to the dark, glassless slot at the top of the front door of the Ford.

A car rolled between them. Rapidly and down the hill. Windrow heard it stop at Corbett, then turn left, drive down the street below him, and disappear down the hill. But he didn't take his eyes off the Ford.

Then it came. He saw a small, diffuse orange glow, behind where the steering wheel would be, and then the smoke. A thin wisp of smoke that was sucked out of the cracked window and up into the fog.

He waited a few more minutes. He used the time to inspect the back of the Trimble house. He was crouched on the deck he'd looked out on when he'd first visited here. Through the sliding glass door he could make out the back of the couch, a corner of it; and beyond that, though obscured in darkness, stood the floor-to-ceiling bookcase, a lower shelf of which, toward the middle, contained his objective. Only the slider provided access to this deck. The deck ran the length of the back of the house. At the other end there was a duplicate window and door that matched the one in front of Windrow; a fixed window, about seven by-three feet with a glass door that slid behind it to open, same size. Between, in an expanse of rustic siding, a small window was set into the wall about four feet off the surface of the deck. Windrow guessed that this was a bathroom. He pulled on his gloves.

The three locks represented the three chances he'd have to gain entrance without breaking something.

Rested, he crawled on his hands and knees to use as much of the railing for cover as possible, and looked closely at the living room door. He could see no wires or sensors, so he tried the handle.

It slid open so easily he almost banged it against the stop at the other end of its track.

Delighted, he could hardly contain himself. His mind quickly flashed the message that he was walking into a trap, but he knew a trap, if sprung by someone other than the police, would be even better than finding some little shred of evidence. If he got out of it, that is, in good enough shape to do something about it.

But he didn't smell a trap. All he smelled was furniture, a little stale perfume, or maybe stale flowers, stale tobacco smoke, dust; the odors of a room that had been shut up for a while, through which no air had circulated. The air was only a little warmer than that on the outside. Carefully, he slipped through the entrance and slid the door quietly to behind him. His eyes adjusting to the dark, he shifted their gaze about the room. Everything was there that he could remember: the shiny booze cart to his right, the sofa in front of him and turned away. Against the wall to his left, a table, and behind that began the shelves of books.

He could hear no sound. He stood up, making no sound of his own. Carefully, so as to disturb nothing, he made his way across the room, to the bookshelf. He tried to remember where the she-Trimble had found the scrapbook. She'd had to lean over a bit, to the second or third shelf from the floor. She'd been standing to the right of the corner table, almost in the middle of the span of shelves. He put his fingers on the place. Their touch brought back to him the

91

memory of the other books he'd seen surrounding the album. There'd been a set of reference books, about four or five of them, each thick and bound in dark green material. These his hands found and counted, four of them. On the other side was a run of unbound materials, magazines or possibly music. Finding these, his hands slid over them and back toward the place where the album had been on its shelf. His hands found the leather-bound set of books again. They backed up. There was a section of loose books, where some of the unbound materials had fallen away from the rest of the sheafs and leaned against the last volume of the upright bound set of four. His hands shuttled back and forth. Bound, unbound, bound.

Sweating again, Windrow found his penlight and risked its small circle of illumination. The light showed him he had the right place. There on the left were the four green, vellum-bound books with gold titles. On the right was a long row of loose folders, apparently typescripts, sheet music, some in folders and paper boxes. In between the two sets of material was a space of a certain size. Windrow put his fingers in the space and spread them. Though he hadn't handled the white album, he judged it would fit in the empty slot his fingers made. He'd seen Trimble get the book from there.

He knew he wouldn't find it. Throwing caution almost away, beyond drawing the drapes over the big windows, he used his light and searched the house. Two rooms upstairs, plus a kitchen and half-bath, and two rooms downstairs, plus a bath. There were a few books around, but not the one he was looking for.

The white album was gone.

Chapter Fifteen

He had a long time to think about it. The fifty-foot nylon cord made it easy enough to get back to the ground and from there it wasn't much trouble to get over the fence, thence the pavement. Going down the hill he woke up a few dogs, but they were all locked in their garages, and the real work didn't start until he got to the lower end of Corbett Street where it intersected Seventeenth. From there it was straight up, one of San Francisco's steeper hills, to get back to the intersection of Seventeenth and Clayton Streets. The traffic on Seventeenth Street was usually pretty heavy, but by the time Windrow had managed the ten nearly vertical blocks to his car, a passerby might easily have noticed the strange figure, dressed in black sneakers and a huge, oversized coat, sweating and cursing its way up the hill, with the occasional clink and clank of hidden metal objects. He might easily have been noticed because he was the only pedestrian on the street. The traffic had diminished considerably; it was a week night and when Windrow opened his car door the first thing he saw was his watch, which had stopped at 12:55.

Yes, he had plenty of time to think about it. He sat behind the wheel of his Toyota, sweating profusely in the overcoat, and turned on the radio. Music from the forties wafted into the little car's interior, and the windows fogged. The man with the soothing voice came on and told Windrow he was alive at home or in his car at 1:33. Windrow started the car and swabbed the windows, inside and out until he could see well enough to drive.

He drove through the Haight-Ashbury on Clayton Street turned downtown on Oak until he got to Filmore. He turned left on Filmore and zigzagged a couple of blocks right, then a block left to a parking space, into which he quietly slipped the little Toyota.

He was parked directly in front of Harry Feyn's house.

There were a few lights on, two upstairs and one in the entrance hall. The porch was unlit but Windrow had been there once before, on a clearer night. Feyn's house was a run-down Victorian, three stories high counting the garage level, which was below the entrance staircase and off to one side. The entire neighborhood was dilapidated. Bottles and newspapers lined the gutters, and here and there a stripped car perched on cinder blocks in a normal parking space. The building two doors down from Feyn's home was burned out, Windrow could see the black, empty eyes of the two upper-story windows, and the shattered timbers sticking out of them. Feyn had bought cheap, and left it looking that way, on the outside, at least.

Though there were several lights on in the house, Windrow couldn't make out any sign of life. As he watched a brand-new white Cadillac turned the corner at the top of the block and cruised slowly down the street. It passed him and drifted through the stop sign at the lower intersection into the bus zone on the other side. The face in the passenger window hadn't missed Windrow's presence, but had sized him up as meaning nothing in its own scheme of things.

Windrow casually noted in his rear view mirror a female figure, black and very scantily dressed, skip out of the building entrance that faced the bus zone and climb into the backseat of the Cadillac. The car idled there for a moment then its ruby brake lights went off and it slid out of the bus zone and disappeared around the next corner, very submarinelike. This neighborhood would be one that never slept. As if to confirm that thought for him, an old Dodge, shooting sparks and noise, dragged its muffler around the lower corner of the block, lumbered just up the hill from where Windrow was parked, and discharged a man from its passenger side almost without stopping. The man fell across the hood of the car parked in front of Harry Feyn's house, and a sardonic laugh followed him out of the car as it chugged up the block with the passenger door still open. As it rounded the corner at the top of the block, completely ignoring the stop sign there, a metal can was ejected from it onto the sidewalk, and the door closed weakly. The man who'd been dropped off rolled off the hood of the parked car and staggered to the curb using the front and back of two parked cars to hold himself up. He managed to get to the handrail of the stoop next to Feyn's before he gave up and began to yell a woman's name, or rather gurgle it. The metal can rolled down the sidewalk behind him and into the gutter in front of Feyn's house. Windrow couldn't understand what the man was saying, but his persistent entreaties got results. The door at the head of the stairs, behind an iron grillwork gate, opened and flooded the steps with a weak, yellow light. A woman and a young child, possibly a boy, came down the steps, the woman cursing and shrieking at the man as she walked, she in her nightgown, the child beside her saying nothing. The man cursed back at the woman as she led him through a graceless rumba—two steps up and one back—to and finally through a series of complicated negotiations with the self-closing and locking gate. She finally left the child locked on the outside, and took the man inside. A moment later Windrow heard the electric buzzer on the gatelock; the child quietly pushed the gate open and let himself in the front door. The meal gate crashed shut behind him.

Before the yellow light behind the transom window above the front door was extinguished, Windrow could see that there were at least six doorbell buttons on a panel beside the front gate. Yet he had heard no protest at all to the ruckus. No one had thrown open an upper-story window and rained shoes and curses down onto the heads of the noisy family stumbling around on the front steps. He checked his watch: 2:15. The public bars had closed at 2:00.

A shiny late-sixties-model Chevrolet rounded the corner at the top of the block and came down the street jumping wildly. As the back end of the vehicle dove toward the ground, the front end leaped so high in the air that the front wheels almost left the pavement. The rear tires jerked and squeaked as the driver alternately goosed the engine and touched the brakes; the headlights swerved wildly in the fog above the street and sparks flew from the extremely loud and low exhaust pipes. This antic apparition convulsed its way through the stop sign at the end of the block, though it bucked and squatted there for a moment, as if indeed looking both ways, then passed on and disappeared into the night beyond.

Windrow set his jaw. A perfect neighborhood for his operation tonight. Nobody would pay any mind to anything that might happen. Grimly, he pulled his .38 from its harness where it lay on the floor and put it in a pocket of his overcoat. He found a dime among his change in the glove compartment.

Leaving the car, he walked down the hill and across the street to a darkened store front. A notice-encrusted post held up the entrance to the store, and someone had bolted a pay phone to the post. For some reason, a telephone book was still attached to it. The penlight helped him find the number. Inserting the dime, he watched the upper windows in Harry Feyn's house while he dialed the number.

There was no movement in the house, and no one answered the phone. He hung up, got his dime back, reinserted it and dialed again. Same results. No movement in the house, nobody answered the telephone. He hung up.

He didn't even wait for his dime. He walked diagonally across the intersection and up the block pulling on his gloves. When he came to Feyn's steps, he took them two at a time, and had the lock on the entrance gate in the focus of his little flash before he'd stopped at the top of them.

The lock was an Arrow, a brand he had keys for. He pulled his ring of passkeys out and found three marked Arrow. The second one fit. The gate opened.

He passed through it and found the locks on the solid-panel front door with the beam of the flash. These were both Schlage locks, and one of them was a deadbolt. He tried his passkeys, and got one of them to turn the tumblers in the knob, but none of them would draw the deadbolt. The doorknob turned, was unlocked, but the deadbolt held firm.

So Windrow broke the law for the second time that morning.

He didn't hesitate. With his flat prybar he opened a crack between the top of the doorrail and the stop, and inserted one of the wooden wedges there. He did the same thing at the bottom of the door. Moving up from the floor, above the second wedge, he inserted another one. The jamb cracked. Above the lock, below the first wedge, he pryed the door back and inserted a fourth wedge. He removed the first wedge from the top of the door, pryed the door carefully, so as not to split the stop before the lock gave way, and inserted it just below the lock. The jamb began to splinter. He placed his prybar an inch above the bolt turned the knob, and the jamb behind the bolt gave way completely with a loud crack.

He was inside.

He pushed the door to behind him and listened for a long time. The house was so quiet he could hear the refrigerator in the kitchen—nothing else. He closed the front door and locked it. The damage to the jamb would be invisible from the outside, and the locks would function normally; their noise should give him a warning.

Windrow started in the living room, to the right of the entrance hall. He didn't bother with the flash, he just turned on the light. Here he found an elegant room. Like many city homeowners, especially in the run-down neighborhoods, Feyn maintained a drab, even shabby exterior, but an elegant interior.

In the living room were walnut bookcases full of fine and exotic books of literature, music, science, the macabre, erotica, and pornography. Many were custom bound. There were etchings, oil paintings, and sculpture where there weren't books; lush, erotic, some of them good, and some of them looked expensive to Windrow, though he wouldn't know. He carefully paced his search through the bookcases. He was after a particular book, and didn't want to overlook it if it were disguised. Feyn was a smart man. He already knew that the photograph album was a valuable piece of evidence. But he would also think that nobody outside himself and Trimble knew about it. Sooner or later, however, Feyn would have figured out that Windrow would suspect what might be in there, and then Feyn would have to face the possibility that the book would have to be destroyed, or at the very least, well hidden. Feyn and Trimble had taken the great risk of spiriting the book out of the Trimble house, which showed that it meant a great deal to them. Windrow was gambling that it was just possible the book meant enough to them that they wouldn't destroy it—yet.

The search of the living room took a long time. Too long. If Windrow didn't come up with the goods before he was caught here, he'd never bluff his way out of a breaking-and-entering rap if Feyn got ahold of a good lawyer. Come to think of it Feyn regularly employed one of the best.

He couldn't find it. Halfway through the living room, Windrow abandoned his methodical search through the two walls of books and went through the door into the dining room. There he found an antique table under a chandelier, a tall sideboard full of displayed china, another oriental rug under it all. No book. He went into the kitchen. It was a Swedish job, all formica and blond wood. He looked into the refrigerator. There was German beer, milk, cream, unground coffee, a lot of vegetables, and several bottles of white wine. He opened a bottle of dark Beck's with his pry-bar and took a long swallow. It was delicious.

He went upstairs. The first bedroom was a guest room, tastefully but sparsely furnished. No books in sight, outside a few magazines on the night table, and no clothes in the closet. Through the connecting bathroom, which looked clean but lived-in, he found the master bedroom. This was a sight he'd rarely seen the like of, with heavily draped windows, a massive stereo system, twenty-five feet of shiny, case-hardened chain piled neatly on the night-stand next to a huge double bed, violently erotic art on the walls, and two closets full of clothes of every description. There were men's business suits, women's dresses, and leather jackets, chaps, vests, pants and boots.

Again, there were lots of books, but not the one he was looking for. He went back into the hall. At the end of the hall opposite the stairhead was a door with two locks on it.

He tried it. Locked. He used his passkeys, and one of them opened both locks.

This was the room he'd seen lit from the street. It looked like a newspaper office. Windrow realized he was standing in the editorial premises of *Brandish* magazine.

The walls were covered with tacked-up layout sheets, originals of cover art without the titles on them, long strips of galleys, drawings and photographs. There were schedules and bundles of paper tacked on top of each other. Against every side of the room there was a drawing board or desk heaped with materials. Piles of back numbers of the magazine were stacked in corners, and wastebaskets overflowed beneath the desks. The room smelled of ink and glue and paper. Two of the desks had typewriters on them.

The white photograph album lay on top of one of the typewriters.

Windrow closed the door behind him and pulled a stool up to the desk with the typewriter and the photo album. He went to the front wall and tried the window there. It opened easily. From it he could look down on the front entrance to the house. He left the window cracked and sat down at the desk, with his beer and the album.

Chapter Sixteen

It was, as he had suspected, chronological. Beginning on the first page of the album, the Trimbles had recorded photographically their lives together. The first three pages were wedding pictures, Herbert Trimble the short-haired young bridegroom, and Honey Trimble the pretty, younger brunette Windrow would never meet. They looked happy and enthusiastic. There were pictures of relatives, though not a full complement of them. (One father and one mother seemed to be missing from the family group pictures.) The wedding had evidently been small, and most of those in attendance had been young friends of the bride and groom.

There followed many pages of photos of parties, of award

ceremonies, picnics, of convertibles full of people parked in front of fancy restaurants and on beaches. Every few pages there was a formal portrait of a chamber ensemble or small orchestra, featuring Herbert with his cello. There were a few yellow clippings. One announced the Trimble's engagement, another their wedding. Two or three told of an orchestra's triumph and mentioned Herbert, among others, as outstanding.

Then a few shots showed up of Herbert standing in front of or knee-deep in holes in the ground, surrounded by people in pith helmets and knee shorts. In one such shot a skeleton was laid out on the ground in front of the crew. Everybody squinted in the sun. In another shot a similar crew was surrounded by all sorts of broken pottery and pieces of tools and bones. The museum days.

Then an odd one showed up. It was a shot of Herbert wearing women's clothes, looking shy, but coy. After that the usual stuff again, until one showed up of Honey wearing only a bizarre selection of black underwear. She didn't look too happy in the overlit glare of the flash.

Windrow sipped his beer. Now the photographs began to be only of social gatherings, of parties that got to be wilder and wilder by the look of them. The people involved had new faces, and many of them were bleary-eyed and expressionless. The number of familiar faces, the ones from the museum parties, the orchestras, and wedding pictures, dwindled. When they did show up, among the aggressive and drunken faces of the new round of acquaintances, the old friends looked disapproving or wooden or confused. The Trimbles were heading for a decadent style in which their old friends took decreasing interest. As the pictures continued, the photographers' attitudes changed. They seemed to delight in catching people in awkward or silly postures. And the Trimbles must have kept them all. The book was crammed with photographs of people sitting in each other's laps, of men kissing, of swimming pools full of people floating with all their clothes on, heads being doused in punch or champagne or beer, people blowing pot smoke at the camera.

Then costumes appeared. Everybody at all the parties wore costumes. Men dressed as pirates, as ducks, as women; the women dressed as nurses, as pirates, as men. The costumes got scanty, and people began to tear them off of each other. There were shots of men and women including both Trimbles, barely dressed in shreds of clothing. Herbert looked deliriously happy; Honey looked, as before, as if she weren't too sure.

Now and then a completely normal shot would crop up. One of Honey in her flowering garden, smiling; another of Herbert shaking hands and accepting what looked like a check from, ah—Harry Feyn.

The parties got wilder, and Harry Feyn figured in many of the photographs. A large color print turned up of the swimming pool again. The pool was lit and the picture obviously taken at night. Everybody in the picture, in the pool and out, was naked. There was an air of relaxation in the shot. No one was tearing their clothes off anymore, or throwing drinks at anybody, or pitching fully clothed people into the pool.

Then the shots went indoors. The people were naked still, and embracing. First shots were of heterosexual couples embracing or sitting in each others laps, smiling at the camera. Then the quality and the content of the photos suddenly changed. A high-class photographer had shown up. The pictures were in color, perfectly focused, well composed. The people involved were openly engaging in sex, no longer paying any attention to the photographer. Many of the shots involved single people in erotic poses. There were several of Harry, and several of Herbert and a few of Honey, and several of people Windrow didn't recognize. Excepting Honey, they generally looked like they were having fun.

The faces were changing again. The Trimbles were on a road that had no end as far as they were concerned. It looked like Herbert was in charge, and Honey wasn't sure. But she was always there.

The pictures of group sex and the quality of the photos fell off again. Many were blurred, out of focus, badly lit. The groups numbered up to fifteen people. Windrow saw all the

101

kinds of sexuality in these pictures he'd ever heard about.

But it was none of his business. Not yet. He skipped ahead. He scanned the faces in every photograph, looking for one he might recognize. One finally came.

It was a shot of the museum staff standing in front of the kind of table and curtains you might expect to find in a banquet room in a motel. The photograph had been done by a pro, with copies going into the annual report and to everyone involved. This copy had been clipped from the report, with its caption:

Pamela Museum Annual Staff Banquet. (1 to r) Sheila Smith, Sec.-Treas.; D. Stanton, Mus. Vice Chair; T.I. Hoople, Mus. Chair; A.M. Johnston, Mus. Cur.; H. Trimble, Ass. Cur.; W. Schwartz, Ass. Cur.; S. Driscoll, Acc. Cons.

Windrow stared at the face. Big features; short, straight hair; thick lips; big ears. Eyes close together. A big man Driscoll was, physically outstanding among the museum staff; he would be about Windrow's size. Except for the ears. The guy had big ears.

Peering closely at the picture, it looked to Windrow as if Trimble's head had been turned toward Driscoll, but he'd gotten his eyes around in time to look at the camera over his smile.

Everyone in the picture was smiling, except for Driscoll. He had no expression and dull eyes. Windrow wondered what it would take to light them up.

He turned more pages. The poses and manner of dress went kinkier. The parties got smaller. Black leather undergarments started to show up. Windrow spotted Driscoll, Feyn, both Trimbles at a party. The background was Feyn's living room.

Then the wall turned up for the first time.

It was the same picture the she-Trimble had tried to hand Windrow. It had been thrust back into the book without being remounted. Windrow picked it up. Beneath it was a picture of the real Honey Trimble. She was draped from the shackles, with a glazed look in her eyes. Her mouth was open, and a little trickle of something dark ran from it. On the next page was a shot of Trimble himself. He was dressed as a woman, his clothes were in shreds. Dark, thick stripes showed on his exposed flesh. He, too, looked dazed, yet there was a hint of a smile in the line of his mouth. Then a picture of Feyn turned up.

And then—nothing.

There were a few pages left in the book, but they were empty.

Windrow finished his beer and thought a moment. The pages of the album were made so as to receive the photographs onto a gummed surface, over which a thin, transparent plastic sheet dropped and stuck into place to protect the photographs. The pages were bound in the book with a spiral wire of many turns. He held up the book, still open where he'd stopped, and shook it. A few little shreds of paper drifted out of the spine and down to the desk. He examined them closely. They were bits of the same paper the pages of the album were made of.

He turned to the back of the book. On the inside back cover a little label in the lower-left corner declared in swash italic script that this Hamborg portrait album was made of the finest materials available, without regard to cost. Below that in tiny print: BDT-10010, 100 pages. Windrow counted the pages. They numbered 48. That meant the manufacturer counted each side of each page, 50 pages gave 100 individual sides.

Which meant four sides were missing.

Windrow stood up and paced the room. Once, twice, three times. He stopped in front of the desk again. It looked like the one of the four in the room that Feyn used for business. There was a spike with bills on it. There was a desk organizer full of mail and catalogues and lists. There was a checkbook.

Windrow opened it up and ran his finger down the list of disbursements. Nothing seemed to be unusual. There was a check made out for the light bill, one for the car repairs, another to a printshop, one to a lithographer, another to a

103

stationer. Feyn obviously ran everything through his magazine business. None had been written less than five days ago.

But a deposit had been made, just yesterday, a big one. Five thousand dollars, less cash four thousand. It was labeled "Brd Ad."

"Brd Ad?"

As he stood pondering the possible vowels that might fit in between these consonants and make sense of them, he heard strange noises.

They came from far away, possibly from another building.

A car went by slowly. The streets were beginning to be wet from the fog, and the cars' tires hissed in the moisture. He couldn't hear the unidentified sound anymore.

But when the car had turned the corner and was gone, the curious strains came back.

They were made by the bowed strings of a cello.

Some of the notes didn't reach his ears, but he was sure of it: They were the notes of a cello. And it was a sure thing they weren't coming from next door. They were coming from somewhere in Feyn's house. At that time, Windrow knew only one cello player.

Very quietly, he returned the checkbook to the desktop, and picked up the white album. He left the room, shut the door and locked it, taking care to make no noise. The cello was still playing, but it was no louder in the hallway than it had been in the office. He walked softly to the stairhead and down the stairs. He had the album in one hand and his other on the gun in his pocket. One tread creaked.

Downstairs he could find no one, but the cello, though still very faint, was louder in the kitchen than anywhere else. He looked around, and behind the kitchen door he found another door he hadn't seen before. When he opened it, the cello got a little louder.

Wooden stairs led away from him into the darkness of a basement, perhaps the garage. He clicked on his penlight and followed them down. They landed on a concrete floor. The little disk of light in his hand showed boxes, hand tools, a bench, dusty furniture. Behind them all, toward the back of the house, his light found a door. The music was loudest there, but not so loud as he thought it should be. The door was large and wooden, and no light escaped from behind it. A large barrel bolt seemed to be the only thing securing the door. Windrow hesitated. Tucking the book under his arm, he drew his pistol out of his pocket and pulled back the bolt with the hand that held the flash. Grasping the knob, he pulled the door open.

Another door stood behind the first one. This one was also made of wood, covered with foam and black burlap, and opened away from Windrow. The music had gotten louder yet, but still not as loud as it should have been, had someone actually been playing a cello immediately beyond it. Windrow recognized that he was letting himself into a sound-proofed room. He examined the door jamb with his flash. It would be at least eight inches thick.

Quietly, he slid the restraining bolt out of its socket and turned the knob below it. The door opened. He pushed it so that it folded all the way back on its hinges, against the wall behind it.

Herbert Trimble sat on a bench against the far wall, playing the cello.

He looked terrible. He had a black eye. His hair was ragged. But his good eye had enough mascara and eyeliner on it to make it look almost as bad as the bad one. There was rouge on his cheeks, a sort of peach color, and he had on lipstick, a bright, crimson lipstick. But he hadn't shaved in a couple of days, or his depilation compound had failed him. Stubble of black beard poked through the thick surface of makeup on his jaw and cheeks, and the lipstick was crooked and badly applied, as if done hurriedly and without the advantage of a mirror.

He had on the same cravat Windrow had seen on him early the morning of the day before, untied, and the same pants, but he wore a woman's yellow summer frock over them. The straps of the frock exposed the bare, thin white shoulders and the stubbled masculine, black hairs growing back on his chest. His underarms had been shaved, but not recently.

105

Herbert had painted the nails of his fretting hands with a polish that matched his lipstick, more or less. On his feet, he still wore the black evening socks and the black Italian leather shoes he'd had on the last time Windrow had seen him.

Trimble stopped bowing in the middle of a phrase and looked at Windrow. "Hello, Mr. Windrow," he said with a strangely friendly smile. He closed his eyes, as if concentrating on something, then opened them again. The pupils found Windrow, and the eyes laughed with the mouth: a short curtailed chuckle. Then the eyes closed again, and the bow hand began to sway in time, and the body made as if to synchronize with it, but no string sounded.

Windrow wondered where the mind was. Still holding his gun on Trimble he stole a glance around the room.

The wall behind Trimble might have been the one in the photographs, but it was covered in wood now, and festooned with shackles and metal rings and chains and hooks. Windrow dropped his eyes to the floor at Trimble's feet. The four-inch drain was there, the same one he'd seen in the picture taken of Feyn hanging from the wall. Against the wall to his left was a door, which he guessed would lead to the breezeway next to the house. Next to it was a table covered with bottles of liniment, makeup, one of brandy; a razor; a many-thonged whip; a porcelain basin; a pitcher; towels. Under it stood a suitcase.

The bench Trimble was sitting on was big enough to use as a palette. Against the other wall were two chairs, and a couple of racks on which hung several different kinds of whips, handcuffs, shackles, lengths of chain, much rope, gags, masks, leather thongs and clothes, and a large, medieval mace, flanked by two halberds. Windrow guessed, or hoped, that most of this stuff was ornamental. But he would never be sure.

"Herbert," he said.

No answer.

"Herbert. Are you a prisoner here?"

No answer.

"Herbert, if you're here against your will, tell me so, and I'll get you out of here."

Trimble suddenly straightened his posture and opened his eyes long enough to look sideways at Windrow. He closed them and, bowing his head, began to primp his hair with his free hand.

"Why, Mr. Windrow," a voice said, "I didn't realize you cared so very much as all that." It was Trimble speaking but it was an affected feminine voice. "If I'd known you were coming . . ." Trimble chuckled, and didn't finish the sentence. Then he said. "You were so . . . so brusque, the last time we met"—he looked at Windrow coyly, through his eyelashes—"I didn't think you cared to renew our acquaintance."

"Last time we met, Herbert, your friend Harry Feyn bashed me over the head with a blunt instrument. I didn't have the time to be properly brusque."

Trimble stopped primping and looked at Windrow with genuine puzzlement in his expression.

"You were *hurt* when last we met?" She—for, Windrow realized, she it was—arched her back. "I'm sure *I* didn't hurt you. I'm always *most* careful in those matters. Hmph. You must have me confused with some other girl, you dog." She winked at Windrow.

Windrow rubbed his cheekbone with the muzzle of his pistol. The guy Trimble was very gone, that was obvious. But Windrow still didn't think this confused creature could have done what was done to Virginia Sarapath. On the other hand, if someone wanted to hang her murder on Trimble, there wouldn't be much trouble getting him put away somewhere for keeps. Nobody would believe a thing he said. They could convict him criminally insane, give him his cello, and lock him up. It probably would happen to him anyway. It looked like Feyn had already gone pretty far in that direction. Why?

"Herbert—I mean, Honey . . . ?"

Honey was straightening the straps to her gown. The cello bow lay forgotten on the bench beside her, the cello leaned near it.

107

"Yes, Mr. Windrow?" Her voice had become theatrically frosty.

"Would you like to come with me, to get out of here, to go someplace safe?'

"Safe, Mr. Windrow?" Honey Trimble frowned and looked toward Windrow, but avoided his eyes. "What do you mean, safe? This is Harry's home, and I feel perfectly safe here."

"You're not worried what Harry might do when he comes back and finds you've talked with me?" Windrow was grabbing at straws.

Honey looked away from him.

"Will he hurt you," Windrow said softly, "when he finds out?"

Honey looked at him fiercely. A tear ran down her cheek. Great canyons of misunderstanding opened between them. Windrow could suddenly see clear to the bottom of them. It meant something.

"Why will he hurt you, Honey? Doesn't he know I want to help you?"

Honey looked at Windrow and bit her lip.

"Why, Honey?"

When the tip of his steel cane pricked Windrow in the back of the head, in the little hollow at the top of his spine, Harry Feyn gave his own answer.

"Because he's afraid, Mr. Windrow," the new voice said.

Had there been an electrical charge on the tip of the unsheathed sword it could scarcely have had a stronger effect on Windrow's nervous system. The tingle raised the hairs and traveled a ways down the top end of his spinal column oscillating from side to side.

"Throw the gun toward Herbert, Mr. Windrow, gently."

Windrow underhanded the gun to Trimble. The latter caught it with surprising alacrity.

"Thank you. Now hand that white book under your arm toward me. Ah . . . thank you." The man sighed audibly. "That's a great relief," he said. "I shouldn't leave these valuable things lying around, especially in this neighborhood. Step forward, Mr. Windrow, if you please. Thank you." Feyn circled around Windrow's left, dragging the point of the sword around the depression just under his left ear. Windrow looked askance at Feyn. He, too, strongly resembled his pictures, except that he was dressed in a three-piece tweed suit. He had short black hair, balding in front, and a neat moustache. His eyes were intense and worried. But Windrow noticed that Feyn kept his back leg crooked a bit and his sword arm bent at the elbow, which was lowered toward his hip. He was set up for a quick thrust, which suggested he knew how to use the unusual weapon in his right hand.

"Now back yourself toward the door."

Windrow did so. The door caught on his shoulder and pushed shut behind him.

Trimble blurted a few words. "He—he wanted to take me away, Harry. He said I would be safe. W-what did he mean? Harold?"

Feyn had backed away from Windrow, who stood quietly. Windrow realized that Trimble had suddenly become masculine again.

"He meant the police, Herbert," Feyn said, "and you know what he told us about the police."

"Who told you? Driscoll?"

Trimble gasped at the name and his head jerked from Feyn to Windrow. He began to mutter and babble. "Oh!" he said. "Sammy, how could you! Oh!" he wrung his hands. "She was so good to us, Harold, so kind . . ." Windrow watched Trimble closely. He was sliding from his male role to his female role and back again. It was too quick a change to be anything but genius or bad mental health. Windrow guessed the latter. Facial expressions characteristic of both sex roles flitted across Trimble's face, singly and in clusters, out of order, like mixed up frames in a movie.

"He's coming apart, Feyn," Windrow said. "He'll be a basket case by sun up. He already is. Where do you think you're going to hide out with this?"

"He's a great artist," Feyn said evenly, "and he's my friend. He'll be himself again, as soon as we get out of town." He opened the door behind him by feel. As Windrow had expected, it led to the waiting night.

109

"You're crazier than he is," Windrow said, "if you think you can hide Trimble safely. How are you going to pull it off? Where are you going to go?"

"We're all taken care of, Mr. Windrow. We just don't want to hurt you."

"Me? You're all taken care of? By whom? Driscoll? I'll just bet you will be. He's already killed twice, hasn't he? Maybe more times than that. You think he's going to stop now?" Windrow gestured at Trimble. "Your friend here may be loco, but the guy that did in Virginia Sarapath is really sick." He turned to Trimble. "Who killed Honey, Herbert? Who killed your wife? Was it you?" Trimble looked wildly from Feyn to Windrow at these questions. He was visibly crumbling under the strain of dealing with Windrow and Feyn in the same room.

"Stop it!" Feyn shouted. "You're hurting him!"

"Who—who, Herbert?" Windrow persisted. "Was it Harry? Was it Sammy Driscoll?"

"Shut up!" Feyn screamed, and he whipped the sword in the air so that it made a deadly noise in front of Windrow's face. Trimble was shaking, visibly terrified, and stuck, as if completely dumbfounded by an impossible choice. A long groan escaped him, a wail so profound, and so devastating that Windrow hardly knew what he himself was saying. Feyn looked desperately from Windrow to Trimble and back again, not daring to leave Windrow to himself but determined to help his friend through the door to freedom.

They all heard the first crash against the door that led to the garage, but curiously, only Trimble recognized it for what it was. He screeched and stood up, holding Windrow's pistol in two hands that shook so badly that Windrow watched him, fascinated, amazed that the weapon didn't discharge; but when Trimble lowered the weapon and pointed it directly at Windrow's chest, Windrow took it for granted that Trimble was about to blow him away. He was about to make a desperate leap to cover the fifteen feet that lay between himself and the mad Trimble, and somehow still avoid Feyn's long, thin sword, when the door behind him splintered and knocked him directly into Trimble's line of fire.

110

The big pistol bucked and roared in Trimble's hands, the recoil knocking him backward against the wall behind him. The load caught Windrow, he wasn't sure where, somewhere in his upper body, and spun him left almost 180 degrees on his collapsing knees. As the red came down over his eyes, he saw that Feyn had disappeared and the door to the alley was closing behind him. He heard the clatter of the sword as it caromed off the door jamb behind him and saw it fall to the floor as, sitting now and facing directly away from Trimble, he heard Trimble fire again and again. The shots went over Windrow's head and although the sounds he heard weren't quite connected with what he saw, he watched big slugs dig up the cloth and blow splinters out of the wooden door. As he sagged to one side, the door sprang open violently again, and only when he saw the uniforms and Gleason's face, did he finally understand what had happened behind him. But when he saw all the muzzles of their guns spitting sparks and smoking, and heard the roar of his own gun being fired and the pugatorial screams of Herbert Trimble behind him, and heard the shotgun boom in front of him—once, twice, and again—he wanted to hold up his arms, palms out toward them, toward them all to tell them to stop, to say: "Time out." He wanted to tell them there'd been a mistake, perhaps two mistakes, but at least one mistake. So he fell on his face.

Chapter Seventeen

The dream was long. In the dream all possible and certified events, factual and counterfactual, swirled around him. The sparks were constant for a time—he would never understand how much time—but they spit and littered his dream world, as if they produced and acted in its disjunct progressions, and they always wound down to long periods of fretful density, characterized by blankness, but bearing the import of something left undone, a step that wanted taking, a message that needed delivering. Or the gun. Its dark muzzle never wavered from his eyes; it opened up and roared dark eternity at him, like the animate mouth of a cave filled with death.

In the throes of this last ministration, he would try to turn over, but the straps held him on his back. Sometimes the night nurse would listen to him and stroke his cheek, so that part of him at least would know that it was not alone. Small comfort. The pieces of him were only visibly joined together in that bed; the synchronicity of them, their unity, was intangible to Windrow, who went two weeks not knowing his name.

When he woke up, they'd gotten him addicted to morphine to keep him quiet. His insurance policy provided him a bed, but not a private one. His delirium kept everybody else in the room awake. Braddock and his committee, through a sympathetic doctor, had him moved to a room of his own, where Windrow would disturb no one, but the morphine continued. When he'd realized what was going on, Windrow decided he liked it. The treatment continued except that they began to decrease the doses. This slight shortcoming, a long, graceful jump shot from half court that arched up nicely, just right, but fell every time just short of the basket, gave him something to think about. Some of the time.

Gleason showed up with an armload of cheap murder mysteries. Windrow tried some of them, fitfully, but soon gave up. Most of them based their ideas of intrigue on international travel, large amounts of money, businesslike brutality, and noserings disguised as logic. The books gathered dust on the bottom shelf of his night table while he stared out the window, listening to his integument knit itself.

Marilyn was there much of the time. To pass additional time they took up an active interest in the Giants, who were a mere fourteen games out. She read him the sports pages, the only section of the newspaper they let him see, and they listened to the games together. She was working nights in a small neighborhood diner on Sacramento Street. In the afternoon she would show up more or less promptly at two and slip him a nip of brandy, perhaps two—she wouldn't bring anything stronger—and he would exercise himself trying to keep from choking on it. The fumes taxed his one good lung, and convulsed the punctured one, but the little taste took the edge off the morphine, helped him get from the twelve o'clock feeding to the four o'clock.

Marilyn was there the day Gleason came in with news.

"They found Feyn. Motel room in Sparks." He looked from Windrow to Marilyn.

Windrow managed to speak hoarsely through his recently dampened lips. "Tell her, too."

Gleason shrugged. "Hung himself. Used a lampcord and ceiling fixture. Maid found him."

Marilyn avoided their eyes. "Do you think—was he—?"

Gleason lit a cigarette. "Did he kill your sister? Bdeniowitz thinks so."

The door opened and the floor nurse stuck her head in. "Please, sir." She pointed. "No smoking on this ward. If you want to smoke—"

"I can go down six flights to the lobby," Gleason finished the sentence for her. He walked to the window, took one long drag, and flipped the butt into the parking lot below.

Windrow managed to turn his head toward Gleason. "Why—?" he rasped.

Gleason stood before the window with his hands in his pockets, looking down into the parking lot. "He mutilated himself," he said "before he did it. It was the same . . . Sort of like . . ." He didn't finish the sentence. Marilyn squeezed Windrow's arm gently.

"They found a straight razor on the floor of the bathroom. There was blood in the bowl. Hell," Gleason muttered, "there was blood everywhere."

A tear ran down Marilyn's cheek. She stared at the edge of Windrow's bed, still holding his arm, but less gently.

Gleason didn't turn around. They were all silent for a long moment.

Gleason rattled the change in his pocket. "Say, Marilyn," he said, pulling the change out of his pocket and examining it in his hand. He extracted two quarters from it. "Would

113

you step down the hall to the machine in the foyer, and get us a coupla cups of joe?" She looked at him. "Please?" He extended the two coins to her.

She looked at Gleason for a moment longer, then took the two quarters from him. Gleason watched her leave. "With cream," he said. "Extra cream." He turned to Windrow as the door swung to. "Gotta have that extra dose of alumae-sala-sody-silicate. Christ, and they call this a hospital."

Windrow looked at him. "What else?" he croaked.

Gleason sat down next to the bed in the chair that Marilyn had just vacated. "Bdeniowitz will kill me, if he ever—"

Windrow narrowed his eyes and barely moved his head.

"They found a picture. It was propped on the little shelf under the bathroom mirror." Gleason pinched his sinuses and scrubbed his tired, birdlike face with his hand. "It was a black-and-white, showed her sister . . . tied, chained I guess, to a wall. She didn't have much clothes on, either." Gleason sighed. "I guess you know which wall, and whose chains," he said. He looked at Windrow and looked away. "She'd been beaten up a little," he said, "whipped by the look of it, though it's hard to tell from a picture. She had this, this kind of . . . dazed expression. It . . ." Gleason's voice trailed off. "Chrissakes, Marty." He stood up and paced back to the open window. "She looked grateful," he said, almost to himself.

Windrow turned his head so that he was looking at the ceiling and closed his eyes. Gleason's voice floated to him through a gathering dusk. "There was another one, another picture pretty similar to the one of the Sarapath girl. We found it in a sheaf of papers in his suitcase. Same shot, same wall, different party. It was Mrs. Trimble. The real one." Gleason fell silent.

A moment later Windrow heard the door swish open. Conversation, the soft, doorbell-like chime of the paging mechanism, the rattle of metal food trays on a rubber-wheeled cart, drifted in from the hall. He fell asleep.

114

Marilyn was laughing. Braddock was there talking, too. "The guy with the ambulance told me you had so much junk in your pockets—all those tools and stuff—when they picked you up to put you on the stretcher, you clanked and rattled, like they were rolling around a coffee can full of bolts. He said they thought they'd been called to pick up a robot. 'Where do we take him?' the driver asked him. 'Silicon Valley,' the guy on the other end of the stretcher answers, 'and step on it.' " Marilyn giggled, and Windrow smiled weakly, his eyes closed.

Gleason handed a cup of steaming coffee to Marilyn. Together they stood and watched the form of Martin Windrow breathing deeply and regularly, a slight husking whistle audible when he inhaled.

"Tell him when he wakes up that Bdeniowitz is real grateful for the tip on the real Mrs. Trimble," Gleason I said, sipping gingerly. "Tell him he's sorry he sent back that bill for the messenger, unpaid."

Braddock showed him the flat black prybar, and pointed to the shiny, teardrop-shaped crease in it. "They gave me this to show to you," he said. "They found it in the breast pocket of your overcoat." Braddock turned the bar over and over between his two hands, admiring it. "Said it was hard to tell, but it seemed likely that it deflected the bullet from a more destructive path through your body, and that in any case it absorbed a lot of the slug's energy." He placed it on the little table next to the head of the bed. "Seems like it might have saved your life."

Marilyn ran her finger along the crease. Braddock looked pensive, steepled his fingertips just below his lips.

"You remember the brand name of that bar?" he asked, musing.

Windrow remembered it immediately. "Wonderbar," he said weakly.

"Wonderbar," Braddock repeated.

115

"Sometimes when he sleeps, the tiniest frown shows up on his face," Marilyn said, watching Windrow sleep.

Gleason eyed the dusty stacks of paperbacks on the bottom shelf of the nightstand. "What do you suppose that's about?" he said absently.

"Something, I don't know. He won't tell me about it but we'll be talking, and he'll suddenly fix his mind on something not in the conversation, some problem he's worrying on."

"Could be he sees now how close he came," Gleason suggested.

Marilyn looked at Gleason. Her arms were folded, and she had a sweater draped over her shoulders. Gleason himself, she realized, had his mind on something else. It was as if he were waiting for something, waiting for Windrow to say something. She returned her eyes to Windrow's gently breathing form.

"Could be . . ." she said doubtfully.

"Did you find a checkbook on Feyn?" He could sit up now. "Or any money?"

Gleason thought. "No, no checkbook. About five hundred cash, though. Why?"

"And just the two pictures? No others?"

"Just the two pictures. Why?" Gleason leaned closer. "What's up, Marty?"

Windrow's eyes fluttered closed. "Oh," he said dreamily, "I don't know, nothing. Just . . . curious . . ."

Braddock patted his shoulder. "You did fine, Martin. Don't worry about a thing. As far as the committee is concerned, you're still on the case."

"You mean, I'm still getting paid?"

"We're taking care of everything."

"Gee . . ."

"Yeah," Braddock grinned, standing in the open door, "gee whiz." He left.

Marilyn watched the door close and turned to Windrow. She leaned over and kissed him on the mouth. A long,

116

lingering kiss. Her fingers toyed with his ear. "Feeling better, darling?"

"Mmmmm," he said.
"Very much better?" she stroked his neck.
"Mmmmm . . ."
"Much, *much* better . . .?"

"Come on, Marty, is there something else? Something you got that we ain't?"
" . . . just . . . cur . . . ious . . ."
"Bdeniowitz says the case is closed, Marty."
" . . . curious . . ." Windrow's voice trailed off. His breathing became deep and regular.

Gleason sat back on his chair. "Fell asleep again." His voice betrayed a trace of irritation.

"Yes," Marilyn agreed.

But only Windrow's eyes were closed. Lately he'd found that he didn't drift off to sleep at the whim of his body's need to rest. More and more, he slept and woke up more or less regularly. Let Gleason think otherwise, it wouldn't hurt him to think Windrow was asleep.

The new book gathering dust on the nightstand was titled *The Collected Love Letters of Feyn and Trimble*, edited by Hanfield Braddock et al., Bat Press. Gleason thumbed fitfully through it.

Chapter Eighteen

The nurse no longer came to check on him every hour or two. They let him sleep the whole night undisturbed and it would only be a week or so before he'd be allowed to go home. A good thing. He'd been in the hospital for nearly two months. The answering machine had probably run out of tape by now.

But at midnight on a Tuesday, Windrow slipped quietly

out of his bed and dressed. He put on the clean clothes Marilyn had brought for him to wear in the daytime, and put the souvenir prybar, still on the nightstand next to his bed, into his belt.

Then he just walked out of the hospital. It was easy.

He had to walk awhile. The bus was slow in coming so late at night. But it felt good to be out of doors after so long a time in bed. He breathed the cool night air of San Francisco deeply, though carefully. He thought the healing lung worked okay; good enough, anyway. The rib had long since repaired itself.

When the bus came he took it to Franklin Street then got out and walked three blocks to Washington. At the entrance gate to the small, modern apartment house there, he found the button he wanted and leaned on it until he got an answer over the speaker box. The voice was sleepy and sluggish and very annoyed.

"Go away or I'll call the cops," it said.

"Mr. Driscoll?"

"I'll give you ten seconds."

Windrow held down the button. Time passed. The voice came back with a click.

"Okay, buddy. The cops are on the way."

"That's too bad, Mr. Driscoll," Windrow said quickly, "because if they find me here, I'm going to have to tell them all about you and Harry Feyn."

Silence. A car, its horn blaring, ran the blinking red light at the Washington intersection on Franklin Street. The horn was loud, but as it passed its pitch lowered enough for Windrow to hear the buzzer on the front-door lock. He pushed on the door, it yielded, and he went in.

The number under the buzzer said 208. Windrow limped up the stairs, favoring his left side. The prybar hung from his right hand.

At the second floor landing he turned right and went to the back of the building, to the door marked 208. He knocked softly.

The door opened a crack. The safety chain was on and the room beyond it was dark. Windrow could see the sleeve of

118

a dressing gown crossing the gap between the jamb and the inside doorknob. Above that half a face appeared, topped by thinning sandy hair. It had thick lips and the eye of a dead fish. The gun would be flat against the door in the man's left hand, over his head.

"Let me in, Driscoll."

"Who are you?"

"I'm the guy who's going to answer about three questions for you, and then you're going to hand over the rest of that four grand you took off Feyn. Who I am isn't one of them."

The man behind the door said nothing.

"When did you take it off him, Sammy?" Windrow spoke softly, but his voice didn't conceal his hatred. "After you used the razor? For that matter, Sammy, when did you use the razor? After you used the lampcord?"

The eyeball visible in the cracked door jerked from side to side. It was looking for a retreat, thinking about the window behind it across the room, wanting to look at it to check on a few details it had forgotten. But it didn't dare take itself off the knowledgeable stranger in front.

Then it stopped jerking around, and Windrow knew, could see the decision. Each time it got easier for the man with this eye, which now fixed itself on Windrow. If this strange man in the passage knew so much, he would have to join the others. There was a simple, effective, and sure way to get rid of animate knowledge; and he would be almost—the eye widened—as much fun as the others had been. But the eye looked past Windrow—was he alone? The eye widened again—yes—and looked back to, almost down on, Windrow, for the eye was contained in the head of a big man.

"Or do you make them watch?" Windrow said very softly. "Not that I care," he added quickly, changing his tone. "I just need a little money, you know?"

The eye, quite dead when Windrow first saw it, was now quite lit up. It smiled and the tip of a tongue flicked between the lips below it and then the lips moved, shaping syllables.

"Ah, yes, Mr. Windrow."

So he knew who Windrow was. That settled a few more things.

"I'd quite forgotten the money." The voice was sly, unctuous. "Please, come in."

The door pushed toward the jamb, and Windrow heard the tap of something hard against the top of the doorstyle, as Driscoll used his gun hand to push the door far enough closed to slip the night chain with his free mitt.

Windrow made his move. He hit the door with all his weight in his right shoulder, until he heard the chain anchor tear off the door casing. Then he kicked. The door flew open. Driscoll avoided being hit by the door; he simply stepped aside, but the sudden blow to the door had popped his gun hand off it up in the air, so that he wasn't quite in position to bring the butt down on Windrow's head. His arm was pointing almost straight back into the room. Windrow straightened up and simply swung the prybar up hard and flat, perhaps a little too hard, and it whanged against the point of Driscoll's elbow. The bar sounded as if it had been dropped on a cement floor.

Naturally, Driscoll yelled and dropped the gun. Before it had hit the floor, Windrow made the bar turn and arc and cut Driscoll a precise blow in the ribs, then landed a meaty left fist square in the middle of the pained expression on the man's face. With a yelp, Driscoll fell into a chair in the darkness behind him, and half out of it grunting.

Windrow turned on the light and closed the door.

He found himself in a small apartment. The walls were white, the wall-to-wall was a brownish yellow. The ceiling had been sprayed on, and glittered. The kitchen, dining, and living areas were all the same room. The bed would fold into a sofa, with some help. Besides the one Driscoll was using, there were two other chairs in the room. A small low table with a drawer squatted between the bed and Driscoll.

Windrow picked up the gun. It was a small .22 automatic. He checked the load in the chamber and put it on the kitchen counter, its safety still off. He laid the prybar beside it.

Driscoll writhed in pain, half in and half out of the big chair. His big, white, fair-haired legs stuck out of the shiny dark blue of his dressing gown. Blood trickled out of his nostrils. He balled himself up, so he could hold his left arm against his side, his left elbow with his right hand, and his face with his left hand. He alternately whimpered and cursed.

Windrow took the entire apartment to pieces. He took the sheets off the sofa bed, removed the cushions, looked in its cracks and under it. He went through every drawer and cabinet in the kitchen. He looked in the bathroom, which was in a closet off the kitchen. While he moved around the room, he talked.

"You were the guy Herbert Trimble found next door to his place the night Virginia Sarapath was murdered. He walked in just in time to watch you help her cut her own wrists, and it was the last straw. It sent him over the edge. He retained enough sanity to call Harry Feyn, on his own phone, before you'd decided whether or not to kill him, too. He handed the receiver to you, and Harry talked you out of it. Something like that."

Driscoll propped himself up in the chair, still holding various throbbing parts of his anatomy. His expression indicated that he might bawl, like a kid, but it also indicated that his fun was being spoiled, and that he had deep-seated intentions of getting even with the guy who had spoiled it.

"But why? What possible hold could Harry Feyn have over you that would be strong enough to prevent you from eliminating the only witness to a murder you'd committed?" Windrow dumped all the silverware out of a drawer in the kitchen.

"No answer, handsome? That's okay, I already know. The answer is that Harry Feyn knew you killed Honey Trimble. In fact my guess is he could prove it. Another one of my patented guesses is that it happened in Feyn's basement, as a result of a bondage session that went too far." He emptied another drawer onto the countertop, full of napkins and candles, wooden spoons, and a spatula. "Am I warm, Sammy?"

Driscoll suddenly spoke. "She asked me for it," he said in a flat voice. "She begged me for it."

"Yeah, sure, Sam. Just like the Sarapath girl begged you for it. Everybody secretly, way down deep inside, wants to die in extreme agony. Right?"

"You'd be surprised, you, you *creep*." Driscoll said the words as if he expected violent retaliation from Windrow for using it. Windrow looked at him. "How long you been sick, Sammy?"

Driscoll, still holding his elbow, but sitting up straight now, looked surprised at the question. Then he laughed a short, chopped laugh through twisted lips.

"Feyn looked like a smart man," Windrow said. "But for some reason, he was a sucker for your act. He liked you enough not to turn you in for killing Honey Trimble, even though he could prove that you'd done it. He liked Herbert Trimble enough to take care of him, even though, after the second murder, he went right off his nut. What a guy. He was running a regular halfway house. He should have dumped the lot of you.

"And he must have considered it. But then of course it wasn't all that simple, because he was an accessory. Am I right Sammy? Then you showed up with the Sarapath girl, a new—what would you say—a new pleasure victim? And he let you use the facilities. Life went back to its premurder frolics in the old torture chamber, didn't it? Just like old times.

"But Feyn saw what was going to happen. The police found two photos in Feyn's motel room. Of course you planted them there, after you killed him. But they showed Virginia and Honey in about the same state of—what? pleasure? pain? shock? What would you call it Sammy?"

"Ecstasy," Driscoll hissed. The light was back in his eyes.

"Right. Ecstasy. Well, the other side of those pictures is what was behind the camera. What did you look like when those two girls were tied up on the wall?"

Driscoll said nothing.

"Feyn saw it. He didn't catch it the first time around, being the liberal sadomasochist he was. Before he could do anything about Honey Trimble, it was too late. But when things got to about the same level again with this new girl, with Virginia, Harry blew the whistle. He threw you out."

Driscoll was looking at the window and breathing short, sharp breaths. Windrow crossed the room and opened a closet behind the front door. The closet was full of clothes, shoes, and boxes, the contents of which he began to examine systematically.

"The only real mistake he made as far as Virginia was concerned was in not telling her what was going on. Or maybe he did. At any rate," Windrow began dumping the contents of boxes on to the floor, "you finished what you had started." He patted all the pockets in the clothes hanging from the rack.

Windrow turned around and faced Driscoll, hands on his hips. He surveyed the room.

"Did you have any idea Virginia Sarapath lived next door to Herbert Trimble?" He looked at Driscoll. "No, I guess not. Did you know that Herbert was going crazy in public? That Harry had lost control over Trimble, to the point where Trimble went to a lawyer, disguised as his own wife, to file for a divorce from himself?

"How can you explain behavior like that? Trimble would do anything for Feyn, and vice versa. They were somehow in love, those two. And when Feyn made Herbert promise not to go to the law about Honey, not to tell anybody, Herbert promised. But his brain went flippety-flop, and figured out a way to help the world catch on without actually telling it, without pointing the finger himself. In the beginning the problem was, simply, Herbert was too good. He made a great chick. He fooled everybody"—Windrow jerked a thumb at himself—"even me."

Driscoll snorted.

"Eventually, all that bizarre behavior would begin to make sense. People would begin to catch on. But you killed Virginia Sarapath first.

"When Herbert caught you at it . . . Why did you leave the door unlocked, Sammy? You really think you aren't crazy? Maybe not. Maybe you're just dumb."

Driscoll continued to say nothing. But Windrow could see

his body working itself up. He could see the muscles tensing under the bathrobe, a little tic in Driscoll's face.

"So Feyn needed money. He wasn't a blackmailer, although when they get things untangled it's going to look that way. He just hit you for the money he thought he would need to get Herbert to some place quiet and out of the way, where he could play his cello in his own little cello-land, and wear calico dresses if he wanted to, and be of no harm to anybody. Since it was you that was causing all the angst Feyn saw no reason why you shouldn't foot the bill. He'd washed his hands of you, but you'd forced your way back into his life. Your presence was a threat to his other charge, the only one he had left, and Herbert was a threat to you. So why not spend a little money and make everybody happy? What's it for, anyway?"

While he was talking, Windrow let his eyes roam around the room. He'd searched everywhere and hadn't found what he was looking for, but he felt sure that it was in the apartment somewhere. He kicked idly at the clothes and open boxes of records and bookkeeping materials on the floor at his feet.

"When did you first get the idea for the frame, Sammy?"

Driscoll eyed him coldly.

"It was just an ideal state, at first, wasn't it. If only there were some way to just get rid of Feyn and Trimble, all your troubles would be over. You could just merrily go on torturing women to death, exploring every nuance, every sensation, every avenue, every possibility of pain and pleasure and death. You would surpass Trimble and Feyn in your knowledge and skill. The men who introduced you to these unknown thrills would become mere dilletantes. Your teachers would become your students—if they stayed alive to witness it.

"I think it must have first occurred to you when you were in Trimble's apartment, the night he disappeared. You put a smudge of Virginia Sarapath's blood on his door. *Inside* his apartment. Just that one touch should have been enough. But you know what, Sammy? I think that was a whim. I don't think you cared whether Herbert got framed or not. It was the money that pushed you over the edge. For Herbert Trimble it was torture and death. But for you, money. When Feyn asked you for five thousand bucks, you saw red. When he endorsed that check from you, he signed his death warrant."

Windrow paced to the kitchen and then back to the middle of the room. He had his arms folded around him, and hoped that Driscoll hadn't noticed his slight limp. At one point his vision blurred, just a touch, and he hesitated in his speech. He looked at Driscoll. The big, revealing eyes were on him. They missed nothing. They remembered the pain this man had caused them and recognized the danger he represented. The tongue flicked out over the big lips, looking for the taste of revenge. The eyes wanted satisfaction. But they would never know it.

Strange, this big, silent man. Windrow wondered how in the world Trimble and Feyn had ever taken him into their confidence. How had Honey Trimble or Virginia Sarapath allowed themselves to be shackled to a wall by this big, dangerous, silent man?

Driscoll had his feet under him now, and his hands away from his injuries. Windrow doubted whether the gun on the counter, had he it in his hand, would stop Driscoll from springing at him, from trying desperately to retrieve his freedom from the brink of disaster. Driscoll had gotten away with it. For two months he'd thought himself safely away from all harm. The two men who threatened him were dead. One had been accidentally gunned down by the police. The other, Feyn, Driscoll had trailed to Sparks and taken care of with his own hands.

"You were outside Feyn's house that night, weren't you, Driscoll. You were ready to kill them both. I fouled up that plan, but the police fouled me up. They spotted me at Honey Trimble's house and followed me to Feyn's house. I was looking for that white picture book. When I didn't find it I knew that's why Herbert and Feyn had been there the day after Virginia's murder. They had to have that book to protect themselves from you, and it would be just as well if the police never saw it, too.

125

"The cops had searched the joint but they didn't know what to look for. Herbert, in his insane scheme, had shown me what to look for. The white photo album. You see, Driscoll, how Herbert Trimble winds up being the architect of your fate. He showed me what I needed to put myself on your trail. You're a gourmet of sensations, Sammy. How do you think Herbert would feel now, seeing us here, cozy like this?"

Windrow eyed the gun on the kitchen counter, about ten feet from where he stood. The light in the room, coming from an overhead fixture, seemed to him to brighten, then dim again. Since he'd crashed the door, pain had begun to haunt his lower chest where the bullet from his own gun had entered it and punctured his lung. He'd been on his feet for two hours, a longer time than he'd spent out of bed in two months.

Then he remembered the little table, in front of Driscoll's chair.

"The book was in Feyn's basement that night, Sammy. I took it there. Feyn left with it and the cops never found it."

The big man watched him with the eyes of an incensed animal. Windrow took one step to his right toward the kitchenette and turned back.

"Open that drawer in front of you, Driscoll."

Driscoll's eyes blinked. He didn't move.

"Come on, Sam. Maybe then it'll all be over."

Driscoll's lower jaw sawed back and forth under his front teeth. He pulled the drawer halfway open, not taking his eyes from Windrow.

Windrow saw what he was trying to do with the eyes. He was surprised that Driscoll thought it would work on him. He let his own gaze drop to the half-opened drawer. He saw there a corner of a thick, white, leatherette book. So Driscoll hadn't been able to bring himself to throw it away.

"So you had to keep it, Sammy. And the four extra pages"—Windrow let his gaze slide back up to Driscoll's eyes—"did you put them back in, just so? In their proper order? Except of course, you'll be missing the two shots you had to leave behind in Reno." Windrow nodded. "It must have been a tough decision, choosing to abandon those two choice pix, after all the trouble everybody had gone to over them, not least of which was contributed by the subjects themselves . . ." But something changed in Driscoll's eyes. Windrow dropped his gaze to the drawer again and he saw why. After having exposed the white album Driscoll had begun to slowly pull the drawer further open, and the handgrip of a large pistol had come into view. It would be a revolver, Windrow thought. Driscoll's other hand was stealing imperceptibly along his naked knee. The hand had about fifteen inches to go.

Windrow's eyes jumped back to Driscoll's and he recognized the light in them now. It was the gleam of the anticipation of triumph you might expect to see in the eye of the gladiator towering over a broken and downed opponent. The expression contained, too, a queer look. It seemed to ask permission of Windrow to make the move that might end his life.

It was a long way to the little automatic on the countertop. Windrow didn't even know if the thing would fire, whether he could get to it in time, or how it would shoot.

He didn't turn around to measure the distance or to fix the location of the piece. He had that information.

Go ahead, his eyes said to the other pair of eyes in the room. *Go for it.*

Driscoll went for it.